"GET BELOW THE CLOUDS! GET DOWN!"

Pepper saw nothing but grayness out the windows of the plane. Gazing in horror at the pilot, she realized he was frozen by terror to the control wheel. The instrument panel displayed a descent of over fifteen hundred feet per minute.

Pepper tried to right the plane, but his hold was a death grip and she couldn't budge the wheel in any direction.

"Let loose! Let go!" she screamed, pounding on his arm. But he just sat there like a statue of granite.

Suddenly the grayness vanished as the plane shot out through the bottom of the clouds and the earth came rushing to meet them. . . .

CHASE THE SUN

Great Reading from SIGNET VISTA

CHASE
THE SUN
by
Sandy Miller

A SIGNET VISTA BOOK

NEW AMERICAN LIBRARY

TIMES MIRROR

PUBLISHER'S NOTE

This novel is a work of fiction. Names, characters, places, and incidents are either the product of the author's imagination or are used fictitiously, and any resemblance to actual persons, living or dead, events, or locales is entirely coincidental.

NAL BOOKS ARE AVAILABLE AT QUANTITY DISCOUNTS WHEN USED TO PROMOTE PRODUCTS OR SERVICES. FOR INFORMATION PLEASE WRITE TO PREMIUM MARKETING DIVISION, THE NEW AMERICAN LIBRARY, INC., 1633 BROADWAY, NEW YORK, NEW YORK 10019.

RL 6 /IL 5 +

The poem appearing on the quotation page, "High Flight" by John Gillespie Magee, Jr., is from the book *On This Day* and is reprinted by permission of J. G. Ferguson Publishing Company, Chicago, IL 60601.

SIGNET VISTA TRADEMARK REG. U.S. PAT. OFF. AND FOREIGN COUNTRIES
REGISTERED TRADEMARK—MARCA REGISTRADA
HECHO EN CHICAGO, U.S.A.

SIGNET, SIGNET CLASSICS, MENTOR, PLUME, MERIDIAN and NAL BOOKS are published by The New American Library, Inc., 1633 Broadway, New York, New York 10019

First Printing, June, 1983

1 2 3 4 5 6 7 8 9

PRINTED IN THE UNITED STATES OF AMERICA

For my children:
Ben, Jeff, Phil, Matt, Beth, and Becca—
the best kids in the world!

HIGH FLIGHT

Oh, I have slipped the surly bonds of earth
  And danced the skies on laughter-silvered wings;
Sunward I've climbed, and joined the tumbling mirth
  Of sun-split clouds—and done a hundred things
You have not dreamed of—wheeled and soared and swung
  My eager craft through footless halls of air.
Up, up the long, delirious, burning blue
  I've topped the windswept heights with easy grace
Where never lark, or even eagle flew.
  And while with silent, lifting mind I've trod
The high untrespassed sanctity of space,
  Put out my hand, and touched the face of God.

—John Gillespie Magee, Jr.

1

Pepper Lea McNeil scooted over to make room for her friend Linda on the last seat of the bus.

"Can you believe it?" Linda said as she sat down. "We're officially seniors as of today." She waved her report card in the air as though to verify the fact.

"What I'm looking forward to is this summer," Pepper responded, her green eyes sparkling with excitement. She ran a hand through her short red hair. "My lessons start Monday, and I don't see how I can stand to wait that long."

"If you ask me, I don't see how you can stand to start them," Linda said. She gave a pretended shudder and rolled her blue eyes upward. "Why any normal human being would want to fly a plane is beyond me."

"That's just it," Pepper answered glibly. "I'm not normal. But then, look what kind of family I come from."

"I do blame most of it on your environment," Linda teased. "It's not everyone whose family manages an airport and who has a father and two brothers that are pilots."

"Right," Pepper agreed. "And I can't let Jeff get too far ahead of me."

"I can tell I don't need to plan on doing anything

with you this summer," Linda said in a woebegone voice. "You'll be spending all your free time buzzing around the sky." Tossing her blond hair over her shoulder, she leaned back against the seat.

"Don't look that way. I'll still do things with you. You can always come over and help me work," Pepper said with a mischievous grin.

"You've got to be kidding," Linda said, and moaned. "You'll never rope me into washing another plane, and I'm not about to refuel one, either."

The bus stopped at Linda's corner and she got off, leaving Pepper to stare out the window and contemplate the summer ahead. Everything was working out so perfectly, she could scarcely believe it.

This was the summer she was going to learn to fly! She had to be seventeen to get her private pilot's license, and by her seventeenth birthday on August 20, she would be ready for her check ride.

She was lucky Jeff had decided to go into business with their dad. He would be busy working in the shop when he wasn't attending Spartan School of Aeronautics to get his Airframe and Powerplant license to work on planes. That left her to take over his job at the Big Horn Municipal Airport. She could spend all her time around planes and still earn the money for her lessons.

Pepper was jolted out of her thoughts as the bus braked to a stop by the road leading to the airport. After climbing off, she walked slowly up the tree-lined road. There was no need to rush this afternoon as her lessons and her job didn't start for three more days.

She could hear the drone of an engine overhead, sounding like a swarm of bees. Looking up, she watched the blue and white Cessna 152 as it circled the airport, then cut its engine and glided in for a landing.

Probably Joe Weaver with one of his students. Monday she would be that student, and she already felt bubbly with anticipation.

Pepper walked over to their white frame house first. Her mother wasn't in sight, so she was evidently over at the office working. After dropping her purse on the bed, she changed into a pair of faded jeans and an old T-shirt and headed for her dad's shop.

She went through the gate by the airport, clanging it shut behind her, then entered the hangar through the huge sliding door. The hangar was old, built more than forty years ago, but Pepper liked it better than the new, modern T-hangars. The ceiling was twenty-five feet high, making her feel like Alice in Wonderland at five foot six. There was space for about fifteen small planes, but many of the planes were out today since it was such beautiful flying weather.

Pepper paused to run her hand over the wing of the twin-engine Turbo Commander that belonged to Kendall and Grant, Inc., an oil company near Big Horn. Ralph Connolly was the pilot for Kendall and Grant, but he was going to be leaving soon. His son, Greg, was her brother Jeff's best friend. He was also the only boy in the whole world that Pepper really liked, but Greg didn't know about it. She hated to think about his leaving.

After circling a couple of smaller planes and ducking under the wing of a 172, she entered the door of her father's shop. The pungent aroma of oil and gasoline hung in the air. Bill McNeil was hunched over an airplane engine, his forehead creased in a frown.

"Hi, Dad."

Her father looked up, his blue eyes crinkling in a smile. "Hi, honey. What are you up to?"

"Not much. Thought I'd go find Mom and see if she wants me to start supper or take over for her so she can. Do you have any fields to dust tomorrow?"

"A couple," her father said as he bent over the engine once more.

"Bet you'll be glad when Jeff can do some of the crop dusting for you."

"Sure will."

Her dad looked like a crop duster. In fact, he looked as though he could have stepped from the pages of aviation history. He was tall, lean, and dark, with a swarthy face. Pepper always imagined him with a leather helmet and a pair of goggles, especially when he stepped out of the cockpit of his Grumman Ag Cat.

"See you later," she said as she strolled out the door.

"Okay, Pep."

Pepper cringed a little at the short version of her name. It was what Jeff usually called her. She hoped her dad wasn't picking it up, too.

She was really Patricia, but when she was small, her oldest brother, David, said she looked just like a pepper with her red hair and green eyes. The name stuck, and she'd been Pepper to everyone since. She liked that, though.

After weaving her way back through the hangar, she entered the door that led to the office and airport lounge.

The crackling of the unicom greeted her ears, and she could hear her mother talking to a pilot. "Wind from the south. Active runway—one seven. There is one airplane in the pattern."

"His sweetheart," Betty McNeil said, hanging up the mike as Pepper rounded the corner. "Glad to be let out for the summer?"

"Mom, you've got to be kidding! I've been looking forward to *this* summer since I started kindergarten. Anything you want me to do? Go start supper or do something here?" Resting her elbows on the glass counter that held plotters, computers, and flying manuals, she waited for her mother's reply.

"I have everything taken care of here," her mom said. "Why don't we go make supper together? Besides, there's something I need to discuss with you."

"Fine," Pepper answered absentmindedly. "Is Joe up with a student? I was hoping to see him for a minute."

"Honey," her mother said, laying a hand on Pepper's shoulder. As Pepper glanced up at her mother, she noticed a concerned look in her hazel eyes. "That's what I wanted to talk to you about. Joe handed in his resignation today. He'll be leaving in two weeks."

Pepper stared at her mom in disbelief as the words burned into her brain. "Oh, no! He just can't," she wailed. "Now what am I going to do?"

"It's not going to help to worry about it," her mother said gently. "I've already placed an ad in several papers for another instructor."

"And it could be ages before anyone ever answers," Pepper said, chewing on her bottom lip. "That happened last time."

"Don't give up already. Maybe the two of us can think of something you can do until then. If not, Daddy might have an idea."

"I hope so," Pepper agreed, but she didn't feel very confident.

"Why don't you make a fresh pot of coffee while I file a couple of papers and lock the office door?"

"Sure."

Pepper rinsed out the pot, filled it with water and fresh grounds, and left it perking by the sign on the counter that said, "Coffee—25¢." A Styrofoam cup was sitting nearby for people to deposit their change in.

"Ready to go?" Betty asked, walking back into the lounge a few moments later.

"Whenever you are."

Pepper followed her mother out the door, then trudged silently along beside her. She just had to think of a way to take lessons until they got another instructor in Big Horn, but how?

"Don't look so down in the dumps," her mother said, interrupting Pepper's thoughts. "You've always been my incurable optimist."

"Just because I take after you," Pepper said, managing a smile at her slim, attractive mother.

No one would ever guess that her mom was forty-five if it weren't for her salt and pepper hair. Everyone was crazy about her, young and old alike, because of her cheerful, vivacious personality.

She did a good job of managing the small flight school at the airport. And though her mother didn't have a pilot's license, she had taken a "pinch-hitter's" course and could land a plane if necessary.

While the two of them made spaghetti, garlic bread, and salad a short while later, they discussed some other ways that Pepper might be able to take flying lessons. Unfortunately, none of the ideas was practical.

"Joe's leaving is going to mess Jeff up with his instrument lessons, too," Pepper said as she tore the lettuce into bite-size pieces. "Where is he, anyway? He wasn't out in the shop with Dad."

"Greg had some business to take care of in Tulsa and Jeff went with him."

"I guess they want to spend as much time together as possible before the Connollys move."

"I imagine so," her mother agreed. "We'll all be lost without Greg around. He's just like part of the family."

Pepper didn't make any comment on that statement. Greg might be like part of the family to everyone else, but not to her. She'd felt the same way for the last six years that Jeff and Greg had been friends. And then about three months ago, she'd started noticing Greg as a boy. In fact, the one and only boy she would really care to date. Even if the Connollys weren't moving, her dream would still be hopeless. Greg definitely thought of her as a kid sister.

As soon as they had finished preparing supper, Pepper went to her room for a while. If it hadn't been for the ruffled flower-sprigged bedspread and matching curtains at the windows, her room would look just like Jeff's.

Posters of planes covered the walls. There was even a life-size poster of the instrument panel of a 747. In the corner next to the window hung an airplane mobile that Jeff had given her for Christmas, and the shelf over her desk was filled with books about flying.

On her desk lay the new plotter, computer, and logbook she had already purchased for her first lesson Monday. A lot of good they would do her now, she thought, as a lump rose in her throat.

Flopping across her bed, she stared down at the green carpet covering the floor. She had to take lessons from the flight school in Big Horn, using one of their planes, or she could never afford lessons. She had already calculated all the expenses down to the last cent and it was the only way.

She had planned and dreamed about this summer for years, and one sentence had destroyed it. If only someone would answer that ad right away and come to teach at the school. This latest problem, heaped on to the fact that Greg would be leaving soon, was almost more than she could bear.

Pepper's thoughts were still in a turmoil when her mother called her to supper a short while later.

She and her parents had just begun to eat when they heard voices as someone walked up the driveway. In a moment Jeff and Greg strode through the kitchen door, laughing about something.

"Pull up a chair," Bill McNeil said to Greg. "Looks as if there's plenty for an extra."

"Thanks," Greg said with a broad smile. "We could smell that spaghetti clear from the driveway. I was hoping someone would invite me to stay."

"Don't be silly," Betty said, walking over to the cupboard for an extra plate and glass. "You know you're always welcome here. In fact, I sometimes forget you're not one of my own kids."

"Well, how did it go?" Bill asked as Greg and Jeff heaped their plates with spaghetti. "Did you pass?"

"Pass what?" Pepper and her mother asked in unison.

Reaching casually into his back pocket, Greg pulled out his billfold, opened it, removed a white slip of paper, and waved it at Mr. McNeil. He handed it to Mrs. McNeil, and Pepper leaned over in her chair to look at the same time.

"Greg," Pepper's mother scolded, "why didn't you tell us where you were going today? If we had known this was the day for your test, we could have been rooting for you."

"Wow," Pepper said with awe. "How does it feel to be a certified flight instructor?" If only Greg weren't moving, he could be her instructor and both of her problems would be solved.

"I might be able to tell you more about that when I have my first student," Greg responded, grinning at Pepper.

"Yeah, I suppose so," Pepper answered, moving her spaghetti from one side of the plate to the other.

Though she was proud of Greg and happy for him, his triumph intensified the despair she was feeling over her teacherless state. Here Greg was, only eighteen, and he already had a private, instrument, commercial, and instructor's license.

If it had been anyone but him, she would have been green with envy. She would probably be old and decrepit before she even got a private license.

For the first time that she could remember, Pepper didn't feel like participating in the conversation about flying that was carried on at the supper table.

Jeff was the first one to notice that she didn't have anything to say. "What's wrong with you, Pep? Cat got your tongue?"

"Nothing," she said, still pushing the spaghetti around on her plate.

Mrs. McNeil reached over and patted her on the shoulder. "As you two know, Pepper was supposed to take her first lesson Monday, but Joe resigned today."

Though she didn't expect any maudlin sympathy from Jeff or Greg, Pepper wasn't prepared for the reaction they did have.

The two boys glanced at each other with a strange look on their faces, and then they both started laughing.

"Well!" Pepper said indignantly, banging her fork down on the table. "I don't know what you two find so amusing about that. In case you don't realize it, Jeff McNeil, that leaves you in a tight spot, too. What about your instrument rating?"

She stared at first one boy and then the other, wishing that she could pierce a hole right through them with her green eyes, but neither of them seemed to notice.

"Are you thinking what I think you're thinking?" Jeff asked Greg.

"Sure. You'd give it a try if it were you, wouldn't you?" Greg asked, his dark eyes full of good humor.

"You know I would, but I'm not sure about Pep. Do you think she's game?"

"Oh, for goodness sake," Pepper said in exasperation. "Would you two quit talking in riddles and tell me what's going on? I thought when David left I'd have some peace, but you two are just as bad."

"Actually, you both know she'll be thrilled," Bill said, leaning back in his chair.

"Daddy!" Pepper exclaimed. "Whose side are you on? Now you're acting just like they are."

"I'm getting a little curious myself," Betty said. "In fact, I don't know if I'll be able to dish up the dessert until I find out what's going on."

"In that case," Greg said, clearing his throat, "I'll explain. Mr. Kendall didn't want to lose Dad as their pilot and offered him a higher salary, and so I found out last night we won't be moving after all. I told Mr. McNeil and Jeff this morning, and——"

"And you just got your instructor's license," Pepper interrupted, a big grin spreading over her face, "and you're going to let me be your first student, right?"

"I don't know for sure," Greg said with mock severity. "You'll have to be a little more respectful than you usually are."

Pepper saluted smartly. "It will be hard, but I'll really try. After all, my whole future may be at stake. Can I still start Monday?" she asked, as she went over to help her mother dish up slices of Blueberry Delight for everyone.

"I don't see why not, but you haven't even got your father's approval of your new flight instructor yet."

"No worry about that," Mr. McNeil said. "I know a good pilot when I see one. Now we'll get to see what kind of teacher you make."

"With a student like me, how can he go wrong?" Pepper quipped.

Though she said the words partly in jest, she was halfway serious. After all, it wasn't as if Greg would be starting out with a student who didn't know anything about flying. She had taxied planes to and from the hangar for ages, and had taken off many times when she'd flown with her dad or David.

Everything was working out just as she'd planned, with only one very important difference. Greg was going to be her instructor instead of Joe Weaver. She couldn't ask for anything more wonderful!

She often went flying with Greg and Jeff, and she knew she would be comfortable having him for a teacher. Her dad was right, too—even though Greg was only eighteen, he was an excellent pilot. He was well on his way to becoming the airline captain that he hoped to be.

Pepper hummed a happy tune while she helped her mother clear the table after everyone had finished dessert. She was so happy and relieved that she felt as if she were already flying without a plane as she rinsed the dishes and stacked them in the dishwasher.

The summer was still going to be perfect. And who could tell, maybe Greg would realize that she was a real live girl instead of just Jeff's kid sister!

2

"Hi, Linda," Pepper called as she saw her friend approaching. "I thought you weren't going to be caught at the airport this summer."

"I didn't say I wasn't coming to see you. I said you weren't roping me into helping you." Linda sat down in one of the folding chairs that was outside the door of the lounge and waited for her friend to finish refueling a Piper Cub.

After topping off the last tank, Pepper dragged the stepladder away from the plane and went inside to take her customer's money. Then she opened one of the pop machines, extracted two Pepsis, and went back out to plop down in the chair beside Linda.

"So what are you up to today, if you don't plan to stay and help me?" Pepper asked, handing one of the pops to Linda.

"I'm going to look for a job," Linda answered.

"Doing what?"

"McDonald's is hiring people right now and so is the Dairy Queen. Thought I'd put my application in at both places."

"I'll be thinking of you while I get nice and tan working outside," Pepper said.

"Don't you worry," Linda retorted. "I still plan to

spend plenty of time outside. As a matter of fact, that's why I stopped by to see you. A bunch of us are planning to go to the lake for a picnic Saturday. Do you want to come, too?''

"I may have to work."

"Matt Barnes was hoping you'd be there."

"Oh," Pepper said, wrinkling her nose. "In that case, I think I *will* work."

"I thought you liked him," Linda said.

"He's okay, I guess," Pepper answered in a ho-hum voice. "It's just that there are more exciting things in life than going some place with him."

"Such as flying, I suppose," Linda said with a grimace.

"Right," Pepper agreed. "And don't make faces. I don't look that way about your piano playing. I even came to your recital, remember? One of these days I'm going to get you up in a plane and then you'll understand why I'm so crazy about it."

"Oh, I've always believed you were crazy," Linda said with a giggle, 'but don't count on getting me up in a plane."

When the girls had finished their drinks, Linda stood and smoothed out her crisp blue poplin skirt. "Well, I'm off to seek my fortune."

"Let me know how it goes," Pepper said, also rising.

"You know I will. Talk to you later."

As Linda walked away, Pepper shook her head in consternation. Sometimes she wondered how she and Linda had ever gotten to be best friends. They were such complete opposites. Linda was a really pretty girl who was usually quiet. Her main interests were her music and her steady boyfriend, Jason.

Pepper was much more outgoing. Although she wasn't

bad-looking, she wasn't a beauty like Linda. She had a decent figure, and boys seemed to like her, but she didn't know if she would ever meet a boy besides Greg who didn't bore her to tears. Just thinking about it now made her stifle a yawn.

"If you're that tired, maybe you should cancel your lesson this afternoon."

Pepper looked up to see Jeff standing in the door of the lounge.

She stuck her tongue at him, then followed him inside.

"I came to get Dad a cup of coffee," he said. "What time's your lesson?"

"Three-thirty. I hope Greg is on time."

"When it comes to flying, Greg is the most dependable person there is," Jeff encouraged her before he went back to the shop.

At exactly three-twenty that afternoon, Greg opened the door to the lounge and walked in. He looked neat and cool in a pair of tan slacks and a white polo shirt. His dark hair had been cut since he was at their house on Friday.

"Boy, you sure are dressed up," Pepper said, feeling suddenly sloppy even though she had on new jeans and a new western shirt. She had changed clothes at noon just to look nice for her lesson.

"Being a flight instructor is serious business to me, and looking scroungy might reflect badly on my ability."

Pepper gathered her things from behind the counter. "Well, I guess I'm ready," she said.

"Let's go then."

They walked out to N 4782 R, the blue and white Cessna 152 that they would be flying today. After a cautious preflight inspection, Pepper climbed in on the left side of the plane and Greg on the right.

"Boy, it sure is neat to get in on this side of the plane for a change," Pepper said with obvious enthusiasm.

"I remember the feeling," Greg said. "I hope you don't mind if I use you for a guinea pig, but I'd like to treat you the same as any other student. On the first lesson, I want to take each student someplace nice so they'll think of flying as a pleasant experience. I thought we could fly over to White Horn Cove today."

"You know I already love flying, but that sounds like fun."

They locked their doors and strapped themselves in securely, then Pepper waited for Greg's instructions.

"Go ahead," he said. "You know what to do."

While going over the check list with Greg, she primed the engine, twisted the ignition key, and the 110 horses under the cowling thundered to life.

"Oil pressure, check . . . radios, set . . ." Pepper taxied to the end of the runway and continued the check list, "flight controls, test . . . flight instruments, check . . ."

After finishing the list, she took the mike in her hand. Talking over the radio was the one part about flying that she dreaded, but she didn't want to balk and appear foolish to Greg.

"Four Seven Eight Two Romeo departing runway one seven Big Horn," she said in clear voice.

Pepper gave the plane right rudder, turning it around in a circle to check for other planes. When she was certain that the way was clear, she pushed the throttle in and the plane surged forward. She took a deep breath and smiled to herself as she watched the concrete slide beneath them.

In a moment they were airborne! The distant hills drew close, then dropped away as they soared skyward. Greg's hands had been ready to take the controls, but it hadn't been necessary.

"Good job," Greg said, and Pepper felt as though her heart would burst from pride and happiness.

How could she help feeling the way she did, when she was doing the one thing she loved best? She knew without a doubt that she would never cease being thrilled by the exhilaration of flying.

A half hour of green pastures dotted with ponds passed beneath them before they saw the restaurant at White Horn Cove, situated on a dock at the edge of Fort Gibson Lake. As they approached the grass strip, Pepper cut the power. Greg took over the controls, and they glided gently down like a large blue bird to touch the grassy field with only a whisper.

They tied the plane down close to a 172 and a Cherokee that were parked by the side of the runway, then walked over to look at the lake. It was pleasant to stand by Greg and listen to the water lap softly against the shore.

"Why don't we walk over to the restaurant and get something to drink?" he suggested.

"Okay."

"I'm afraid you're going to spoil me," Greg said as they walked at a brisk pace along the gravel road that curved around the edge of the cove. "You really are an exceptional student since you've been around planes all your life. I'll let you try the landing when we go back."

"Great. Am I ever glad your dad decided to stay in Big Horn."

"Me, too. I wasn't looking forward to leaving, and Mom likes it here. Why don't we take a shortcut?"

Greg suggested, pointing across the grassy knoll separating them from the restaurant.

Pepper nodded and they stepped off the road. Going that way would save them about a quarter mile of walking. When they came to a deep gully with water running through it, Greg jumped over first. Then he reached across and took Pepper's hand as she hopped over.

His touch sent a tingle through her hand. "You're sure different when Jeff isn't along," Pepper commented casually, hoping that Greg wouldn't notice she was blushing.

"How's that?" Greg asked, looking down at her with a smile.

"You and Jeff are always razzing me, but you're really polite when he's not here."

"Like I said, this flight instructor business is serious stuff, but if it will make you feel better, maybe I can give you a hard time while we get our drink."

"You don't have to go to all that trouble," Pepper said with a laugh.

They crossed a long wooden walkway to get to the dock where the restaurant was. Ducks and geese swam at the edge of the lake beneath them. After going inside, they took a seat in a booth by the windows overlooking the lake.

"You know, I'm really hungry," Greg said. "How about you? Think you could eat supper now? I'll buy us both a hamburger and some fries."

"Actually, I'm starving," Pepper said. "All I ate was a sandwich and some chips for lunch. I hope you have plenty of money. I might be able to eat two hamburgers."

"I forgot how much you can eat," Greg said. "I'm

surprised you don't get fat! But it's okay this time, I've got enough money."

"Wow, thanks. I guess you meant it about giving me a bad time."

"I couldn't help myself. You're the nearest thing to a sister I've got. Who else can I tease?"

Greg's words seemed to ring in Pepper's ears as she looked out at a waterskier on the lake. "The nearest thing to a sister I've got." How could she show him she wasn't a sister without being obvious?

When the waitress came, Greg ordered two cheeseburgers each.

"I don't know if I can enjoy eating with all those fish staring down at us," Pepper said when their food was ready. She looked up at the trophy-size fish mounted all around the walls of the restaurant.

"They do kind of look as though they're watching us," Greg agreed. "Just be glad we're eating hamburgers and not fish."

While they ate, she and Greg talked about flying. They both had the same dream of flying professionally some day, but it seemed to Pepper that Greg was already miles ahead of her.

When it was time to leave, she regretted ending their conversation, except for the fact that she would get to fly again. Best of all, Greg had said she could try the landing this time. She was really looking forward to that.

It had been fun talking to Greg, instead of listening to him and Jeff. When those two were together, she felt lucky if she got to stick in a single word occasionally. Today Greg had acted as if he were actually interested in what she had to say, and of course, she could listen to him forever.

Greg paid for their meal, then stopped to read a

notice tacked on the bulletin board by the door. "Look at this," he said to Pepper.

The announcement was for the first annual "Sooner Air Classic," to be held in August. It would begin on the Oklahoma–Arkansas line, go to the border of Oklahoma and Texas, and end back on the starting line. There would be five cash prizes.

"I've always wanted to enter an air race," Greg said. "This sounds like a good one. I'm sure Jeff would be my partner."

"You know he would," Pepper said. Taking a pencil and note pad out of her purse, she scribbled down the address that was given to write for information and handed it to Greg.

"Thanks, Pep," he said, folding the paper and putting it in his billfold.

"Ugh," Pepper said, making a face. "I know Jeff calls me that, but I wish you wouldn't."

"Sorry," Greg said, studying her thoughtfully for a moment. "I didn't know it bothered you."

Pepper felt suddenly flustered under Greg's intense gaze. She dropped her eyes and shrugged. "I don't know why it does, but I really don't like it."

"I know how you feel," Greg said. "My mother calls me Greggie once in a while and that almost drives me up a wall."

Pepper laughed. "I can see why," she said as they headed back for the plane.

The return flight was pleasant, but uneventful. Greg let Pepper try the landing as he had promised. She was too high, and he took the controls at the last moment, making her go around once more. When she finally did a rough, bouncy landing with Greg's help, she felt as if she needed to learn a few things.

"That was a humbling experience," she said as the plane rolled to a stop at the end of the runway.

"You'll have the hang of it in no time," Greg said. "But it's always good to be humble no matter how many hours you've logged. Cocky pilots are the ones who end up dead."

After turning the plane around, Pepper taxied to the gas pumps and turned off the engine.

"Fun's over. Now it's time for work," she said. Handing her logbook to Greg, she opened the door and hopped out. She dragged the stepladder over to the plane and climbed up with the hose to refuel it.

Just as Pepper stuck the nozzle into the tank, she glanced up to see a silver-blue Corvette driving up and parking on the other side of the chain-link fence. A girl climbed out and entered the gate.

She came closer, and Pepper recognized Stephanie Kendall. Her father was the head of Kendall and Grant, the company that Greg's dad flew for. Stephanie had attended a private school in the east and would be going to Bryn Mawr in the fall. Although Pepper had only seen her about three times previously, and then at a distance, she would recognize Stephanie anywhere.

She was the kind of girl that stood out in a crowd. She was tall and shapely, moving with the self-assured grace of a model. Her long black hair contrasted with her creamy complexion, giving her a slightly fragile appearance.

Her clothes, pink linen slacks and a lacy top, looked like something from Saks Fifth Avenue, Pepper thought ruefully as Stephanie came closer. Evidently, she was waiting for someone. She was shading her eyes with her hand and looking around.

When she was about forty feet away, Stephanie waved

and called out, "Greg! There you are. I couldn't see you in that plane."

"Come here and meet my first student," Greg said, stepping out of the aircraft.

Stephanie walked over to the wing and smiled up at Pepper. "Hello," she said in a musical voice. "I think I've seen you before."

"This is Pepper McNeil," Greg said. "Her folks manage the airport. Pepper, this is Stephanie Kendall."

"Happy to meet you," Pepper said. She suddenly felt grimy and conspicuous and rather like a grub worm talking to a butterfly. Too bad she couldn't crawl under the wing and disappear.

She didn't usually compare herself with other girls, at least to worry about it. But she couldn't help doing that with Stephanie. She was the loveliest girl Pepper had ever seen, except on the cover of a magazine. Her large violet eyes gave her an innocent look as she smiled once more at Pepper.

"I'll lay your logbook on the counter," Greg told Pepper. "See you Wednesday," he called back as he and Stephanie left.

"Oh, uh . . . sure," Pepper answered a little belatedly.

She stared after them. After Greg took Pepper's logbook inside the lounge, he and Stephanie walked to her Corvette hand in hand. Greg was looking down at Stephanie and they were laughing about something. Pepper felt a terrible pang around her heart as she watched them. Greg opened the door on the driver's side for Stephanie. After she got in, he went around to the other side and climbed in and they drove off.

Pepper had had no idea that Greg was even dating Stephanie. Jeff had never mentioned it. But by the look of things, they must be pretty serious about each other. Pepper felt almost ill.

Greg was really a nice-looking guy—tall and muscular with dark hair and eyes. He would have women swooning over him when he was an airline captain someday. There was no reason why he shouldn't date a gorgeous creature like Stephanie Kendall. Pepper certainly didn't stand a chance in that case, she thought glumly as she dragged the ladder back to its place. She and Stephanie just weren't in the same league.

The plane they had flown today was kept tied down on the concrete slab close to the old hangar, so she had to pull it in instead of taxiing. After fastening a tow bar close to the front wheel, she pulled it about thirty feet into place and tied it down.

Pepper could feel beads of sweat running down the sides of her face when she finished the task. Wiping her forehead with her hand, she headed for the coolness of the lounge.

Her logbook was lying on the counter and she started to pick it up until she looked down at her hands. They definitely needed washing, so she went to the ladies restroom, flipped on the light, and walked over to the washbasin.

A mirror hung over the lavatory, and Pepper studied herself with disdain as she lathered her hands. The only thing neat about her was her hair. It was straight, cut short in a wedge-shaped blow-dry style, and always looked neat.

Thank goodness, because the rest of her was a disaster. Her shirt was wrinkled, and there was a big smudge across her forehead. She hoped it had gotten there after Greg and Stephanie left. She hated to think how she had appeared to Greg today. It must have been a relief for him to see Stephanie.

Leaning over, Pepper splashed cool water on her face, scrubbed at the dirty spot, then dried with a paper towel. She made a mental note to be more careful with her appearance in the future. Hectic day or not, it was no excuse to go around looking as if she were the survivor of a midair collision.

Pepper finished her work quickly. She was done by five-thirty and went home to join her family for supper. Since she and Greg had already eaten at White Horn Cove, she drank a glass of iced tea while the rest of them ate.

"Tell us about your lesson," her father said.

"I got to take off both times," Pepper told them proudly. "Greg didn't have to help me, either."

"How about the landing?" Jeff asked. "Did he let you try that?"

"The last one. *That* is going to take some practice."

"I happened to be looking out the window when you had to go back around the field," Jeff said. "Also when you bounced in the second time." He winked at their father, and Pepper felt a strong urge to reach over and choke him.

Instead, she pressed her lips in a firm, straight line. "I suppose you've always landed perfectly," she sputtered.

"I happen to remember some of Jeff's landings if he doesn't," Mr. McNeil said with an encouraging smile at Pepper.

"Oh, I know I wasn't perfect," Jeff said, "but I still think Pep wins the prize for the most bounces."

"You might be right," Pepper admitted with a laugh.

"It was nice of Greg to buy you supper," their mother said.

"He did that?" Jeff said. "He's even braver than I thought."

"What do you mean by that remark?" Pepper asked, narrowing her eyes and preparing for a rebuttal.

"Well," Jeff said with a shrug, "when a person considers how much you can eat . . . I'm surprised you're not ready for supper again."

"Just wait, Jeff," Pepper said, wrinkling her nose. "I'll get even. Besides, he told me he was going to take all of his students someplace nice on their first flight. We went to White Horn Cove and then he decided he was hungry."

"I bet he'd like Stephanie Kendall to take lessons from him," Jeff said. "He'd probably take her to Shangri La." That was the plushest resort in Oklahoma.

"What's this?" their mother asked.

"Stephanie picked Greg up in her Corvette this afternoon," Jeff explained. "They've gone on a few dates. Now *there's* some girl—talk about good-looking."

When Jeff mentioned Stephanie, Pepper felt the same heartsickening pang that had gripped her today as she watched Greg and Stephanie walk away hand in hand. It was almost as bad as a physical pain, and left her feeling completely dejected. Just when she'd thought Greg might start noticing her, she'd discovered he had someone like Stephanie to notice instead.

3

The yellow dandelions reminded Pepper of streaks of melting butter as the plane skimmed over the grass. She pulled back on the control wheel to raise the nose, and eased the plane onto the runway in a flawless touchdown.

"Good job," Greg said.

"I hope Jeff was looking out the window this time," Pepper said with a pleased smile.

As the 152 rolled along the concrete, Pepper reached out her hand to turn off the carburetor heat. Evidently, Greg had the same idea, for his large hand came down at the same moment and covered her small one.

"You really are on the ball," he said with a chuckle.

Then, to her surprise, he took hold of her hand, giving it a squeeze. Pepper felt completely speechless, and the tingling in her fingertips made them feel as if they were electrified.

The whole episode couldn't have lasted more than a moment, yet in a way it seemed like an eternity. She could feel her face growing pink and she didn't look at Greg as she busied herself with taxiing to the gas pump.

Greg made her have such funny feelings. She couldn't help it, even though she knew he didn't feel the same way about her. If his hand accidentally brushed hers while he was showing her something on the controls, she became terribly preoccupied with his nearness.

She cut the engine when they were at the pump. Greg hopped out and refueled, then helped her move the plane and tie it down.

"Want a Pepsi?" Pepper asked when they were finished.

"You bet," Greg said, following her into the lounge.

Jeff entered the door from the hangar as Greg and Pepper came in the other way.

"How was the lesson?" Jeff asked, looking at Greg. "Bet you're glad to get your feet on solid ground after going up with Pep."

"She's doing great."

"I hoped you were looking out the window today," Pepper said.

"At what?" Jeff asked. "I saw someone in a 152 do a perfect landing a while ago, but I knew it couldn't be you."

"Very funny, but you managed to get into my good graces with that remark," Pepper said. "Want to join us for a pop? They're on me."

"Sure. I never pass up a free pop when my sister's buying. You're not as generous as you used to be."

"That's the way it is when you start taking flying lessons, right, Pepper?" Greg said. "You have to scrape together every cent you can."

"Boy, that's the truth," Pepper agreed. She extracted three Pepsis from the pop machine, passed them around, then plopped down on the sofa. Jeff sat down beside her, and Greg sat in a chair on the other side of the coffee table. "Speaking of scraping pennies, I think I may have enough for an extra lesson next week if you have the time," she told Greg.

"I could give you one Saturday morning at ten." Greg said. He leaned back in the chair and drank half of his Pepsi in one gulp.

"Super."

"You'd better wear an old shirt for the next several lessons," Greg suggested.

"Sure thing," Pepper said. She leaned back against the sofa with a sigh of contentment and gazed at the shirttails tacked up on the wall of the lounge. Greg was letting her know that she would be soloing before long.

It was kind of a funny custom to cut off a person's shirttail when they soloed, but Pepper could hardly wait until hers was on the wall with David's and Jeff's and the others who had soloed through the Big Horn flight school. Thanks to Greg's warning, she wouldn't be like David. He was wearing a new shirt when he soloed and had had mixed emotions about having the tail cut off.

"Well, I've got to go," Greg said after he drained his bottle of pop. He replaced the empty bottle in the wire rack by the pop machine and headed for the door. "See you guys Friday," he called over his shoulder. Pepper could hear him whistling as the door closed behind him.

He'd probably always think of her as one of the guys, Pepper thought morosely. If Greg had any idea how she felt about him, he would undoubtedly be amused and embarrassed at the same time. She mustn't let him find out.

"Greg's really a great guy, isn't he?" Jeff said, rising to his feet.

"Oh . . . uh, yeah . . . sure," Pepper stammered. She wondered if Jeff knew what she was thinking, and could feel herself blushing furiously at the prospect. Jeff would never let her live it down if he found out.

"You okay?" Jeff asked, looking at her curiously.

"What do you mean?" Pepper asked, swallowing hard.

"Your face is as red as your hair. Maybe you're having a heatstroke or something."

At first Pepper thought Jeff had caught on and was teasing her, but he looked genuinely concerned.

"I feel fine," she said. "Did you make arrangements for your instrument lessons yet?" she added hurriedly, trying to get his mind on something else.

"Yep," Jeff answered. "I'll leave here an hour and half early and have my lesson at International before I go to Spartan's in the evenings. Too bad ol' Greg won't have his instrument instructor's license until the end of the summer. He could teach me and I'd save a little money."

"That would be nice all right," Pepper agreed, thankful that she had diverted his attention. "There's going to be some more people looking for an instructor after tomorrow when Joe leaves."

"I was talking to Dad about that a little while ago," Jeff said. "But he just said Mom thinks she's found someone. She'll know for sure tomorrow."

Pepper was so busy on Thursday and Friday that she didn't think any more about the instructor for the flight school.

They were eating supper late Friday afternoon when Mr. McNeil brought up the subject. "Think you'll be happy with your new employee?" he asked, winking at his wife.

"He's young and inexperienced, but I believe he'll do a good job," Mrs. McNeil answered.

"What's the guy's name?" Jeff asked.

"Greg Connolly," their mother answered with a straight face.

"Man, that's super!" Jeff said. "But I can't believe he didn't tell me."

"You'd gone to town to get a part when he was here," their father reminded Jeff.

"Well, he could have told *me*," Pepper said. "I was with him for an hour."

"Listen, Pep," Jeff said, shaking his head. "A guy doesn't just go and tell his best friend's kid sister something first. That would be almost unethical."

He laughed and Pepper knew he was kidding, but still, she couldn't help feeling deflated.

"You know, I think this calls for a celebration," Jeff said. "Why don't we have a barbecue next Saturday evening? Is that okay with you, Mom?"

"Fine," said their mother, "as long as you take care of the arrangements and cleaning up."

"Are you willing to help, Pep?" Jeff asked.

"Sure, it sounds like a good idea."

"Why don't you figure out the food? Hamburgers and hot dogs would be good. That way the guys can help cook. I'll invite everyone that Greg and I run around with and you ask one of your friends, okay? Let's plan on about ten people altogether."

"All right, but just don't forget that you have to help clean up the mess afterward."

"Don't you have any faith in your own brother?" Jeff asked with an ornery grin. "Wow," he said, glancing up at the clock on the wall of the dining room. "I need to leave for my lesson right now." He left his unfinished plate and went to get his books.

About fifteen minutes after Jeff went out the door, they heard a plane take off.

"Most parents are worried about their kids out driving," Mrs. McNeil said with a laugh, "but we have to worry about ours flying."

"It's not nearly as bad, though," Mr. McNeil said. "There are a lot more crazy drivers out there than there are pilots."

"While we're on the subject of pilots," Pepper told them, "it looks as if I'll get to solo before long. Greg said to wear an old shirt for the next few lessons."

"That's great, honey," her father said.

"So soon?" her mother asked with a slight frown puckering her brow. "Is Greg certain that you're ready?"

"Oh, Mom. I've logged ten hours in the last two weeks. There you were just telling us about this great instructor you hired for your flight school, and now you're wondering if he knows what he's doing."

"I also said he was inexperienced. You're my only daughter and I have to worry about you."

"You don't need to worry, Mom. Greg is the best instructor in the whole world." Pepper didn't mean for her voice to quiver when she said Greg's name, but it did.

She knew her mother noticed, too, because she studied her thoughtfully for a moment. "I'm glad you think so, dear," she said at last, "but I still want you to be careful."

"Mom, *really* you sound just like a . . . a . . ."

"Just like a mother," Pepper's father finished, "because that's what she is. And you'd better be thankful that you have one who cares so much about you, young lady."

"I am," Pepper admitted, "and I'm sorry if I sounded disrespectful, but I don't want you to worry."

"I'll try not to," her mother said as they started clearing the table.

"And I promise to be very careful," Pepper said with a grin.

Pepper kept up a constant chatter about everything besides her flying lessons while she and her mother cleaned the kitchen. There was no way she could keep from sounding funny if she mentioned Greg, and she couldn't bear to have her mother know how she felt about him. As close as she and her mother were, this subject was still much too personal to share.

When they were finished, Pepper went to her room to study for the written part of her flight exam. She could take that whenever she was ready and she wanted to get it over with as soon as possible.

Thank goodness she knew as much as she did about the material, so she wouldn't have the added expense of taking a ground school course. Although, if Greg were teaching it, it would be worth the extra money, she thought dreamily.

After spending about an hour and a half studying radio navigation, Pepper decided that she'd had enough for one evening.

Taking out a fresh sheet of paper, she started making a list of food for their barbecue next Saturday. First she wrote: hamburgers, hot dogs, baked beans, potato salad, pop, ice cream. After considering that for a moment, she crossed out the potato salad and replaced it with chips and dip. She might as well make it as easy as possible.

Jeff did come up with some pretty good ideas at times, she had to admit. She would call Linda tomorrow and invite her. Pepper was already looking forward to the barbecue. Of course, it seemed doubly nice since it was to celebrate Greg's new job.

Wouldn't it be super if he actually noticed her next Saturday evening? But she certainly didn't want to get her hopes up, because that would be highly doubtful. Still, she couldn't seem to stop herself from dreaming about Greg. The more time she spent around him, the more she realized how much she liked him.

Pepper had been serious when she told her mother what a super flight instructor Greg was. He always remained calm and cheerful, yet he was demanding at the same time. He never let her just "slop by" on anything. He was the kind of person who commanded respect.

She leaned back in her chair and closed her eyes as she visualized a flying lesson with Greg. When she pictured his large hands on the controls, she thought once more about his squeezing her hand and a warmth spread through her fingers at the mere remembrance. What would it be like to have him put his arms around her? Kiss her? Pepper could feel her heart hammering in her chest as she opened her eyes.

She walked over to her open window like someone in a dream and stared out at the star-speckled night. Of all the boys she knew, why did she have to pick Greg to like? If she could, she would stop her feelings for him now before she got hurt, but feelings weren't something a person could turn off and on at will.

The sweet scent of honeysuckle drifted in on the evening breeze, adding to Pepper's melancholy. The chance that Greg would ever like her was about as slim as someone successfully flying an SR-71 without any flight training!

*   *   *

All of Pepper's gloom vanished with the sunlight streaming in her window the next morning. She lay quietly for a few moments after she awoke, enjoying the early morning sounds and smells.

When she remembered she had an extra flying lesson that day at ten o'clock, she almost leaped out of bed. In a short time, she was dressed for the day in her oldest shirt and faded jeans. Even though she was wearing old clothes, she brushed her hair until it shone and applied some lip gloss.

Her mother was sitting at the kitchen table drinking a cup of coffee when Pepper came out. Saturday morning was cold cereal day, so she poured herself a bowl and sat down across from her mother.

"You're dressed fit to kill this morning," her mom said with a smile.

"Just doing what Greg said," Pepper said with an answering smile. "I don't want a good shirt cut up. After I solo, I'll go back to my usual glamorous attire."

Pepper was certain that ten o'clock would never arrive, but it finally did. As usual, Greg came right on time. Pepper had already gone out to the plane and was starting to preflight it.

"You look as if you're ready to work hard," Greg said, tossing his things onto the front seat of the plane. When Pepper was finished with her inspection, he helped her pull the plane out to the taxiway.

"How are you doing on your ground school material?" he asked as they both climbed in and buckled their seat belts.

"Pretty good. I've been studying every night. I think I'm about ready to take the test."

"Be sure and take several sample tests, and if there's

something you don't understand I'll be glad to help you. No extra charge, either," Greg said with a grin.

Pepper's heart did a little flip-flop. Greg was always so considerate and thoughtful. "Thanks, Greg," she said. Her voice came out squeaky, but he didn't seem to notice.

Pepper knew from the time she twisted the key in the ignition that this flight was going to be exceptional. Everything seemed to fall into place like the cogs meshing in the smooth-running engine that roared in front of them, hurling Greg and her down the runway.

"Stay in the pattern for touch and go's, Pepper," Greg told her.

Pepper didn't answer, but responded by banking the plane left and keeping a tight, square pattern precisely as Greg had instructed her.

The day was perfect. The wind was only a gentle breeze out of the south—hardly enough for the orange wind sock to give the proper direction. The blue of the sky was broken only by puffs of clouds far on the horizon that looked like sheep grazing above the distant hills.

Pepper's hands seemed to glide as they performed their assigned functions of controlling throttle, trim, and control wheel. It was all falling into place and she knew that today would be the day she would solo.

The turn to the final approach was flawless and she was suddenly overcome with appreciation for Greg's stern demands for perfection. She could see how right it felt to do the job of flying well.

The airspeed indicator was holding steady on sixty-five knots as though it were welded there. She thought she heard a whisper pass Greg's lips, "Good."

As the plane slipped gently past the threshold of the

43

runway, Pepper eased the nose higher until she felt and heard the tires brushing the runway with a squeak.

Giving the aircraft full throttle, Pepper repeated her performance twice more with never a word from Greg. It was as if words would break the spell. But after the third landing Greg spoke only one word: "Stop."

Pepper stopped the plane in the middle of the runway and turned to face Greg. Their eyes met in an unspoken understanding of triumph. Greg clicked off his seat belt, opened the door, and turned again to Pepper. "Do that again for me three more times," he called over the rumble of the idling engine. Then he was gone, striding across the grass to watch her from the ramp.

Pepper stared after him, frozen. She really wanted to please Greg and she had so wanted to solo, but now that the time had come, she was suddenly apprehensive. Could she do it? Could she really fly by herself?

She turned and looked down the runway and felt a surging challenge. Of course she could do it! She grinned to herself and shoved the throttle forward. The plane sped down the runway, and with the same flowing movements of her hands she nursed the craft airborne.

Up she went as though the horsepower had doubled. The plane seemed to spring to obey her commands. At first she was surprised at its responsiveness, but then she remembered Greg's telling her that without his weight along, the aircraft would perform better.

As Pepper made her tight turn in the pattern, she looked around and for the first time saw the world as though she had conquered all the realm below her.

"Whoopee!" she shouted with a grin on her face and a touch of joyful tears. How long had it been that she had waited for this day?

Pepper made her three landings as perfectly as when

Greg had been with her. She taxied the plane to the gas pumps, killed the engine, and jumped out.

"Yippee!" she shouted for everyone to hear. "I did it." Pepper was overcome with the joy of the moment and without thinking when she saw Greg walking proudly up to her she ran to him, threw her arms around him, and once again said, "I did it."

Greg hugged her back, spun her around once, then set her back down. "You sure did, and believe me you looked fantastic!"

Pepper had been too excited before to think about being hugged by Greg, but now she was terribly conscious of his arm still around her shoulder as they walked to the lounge. If only they could walk a mile this way so she could absorb the pleasure of this moment.

"I see you took me seriously about wearing an old shirt," Greg said with a laugh as they went in the door.

Pepper was surprised to find her mother, father, and Jeff, all waiting in the lounge.

"Congratulations, sweetheart," her father said.

"Greg buzzed us on the intercom as soon as you took off by yourself," her mother explained. "He thought we might want to watch you."

"Only thing was, Mom wouldn't look," Jeff said. "She hid her eyes most of the time."

"At least I brought the scissors," her mom said, handing them to Greg.

"Turn around," Greg commanded Pepper.

He whacked off her shirttail, laid it on the counter, and with a magic marker wrote her name and the date she soloed. Then he went over and tacked it up on the wall beneath Jeff's shirttail.

Pepper felt certain her heart would burst with happiness when Greg walked back over to stand beside her and patted her on the back. "This first student of mine is quite a gal," he said with pride.

And her instructor was quite a guy, Pepper thought as she smiled shyly at him.

4

Pepper felt certain that this day had to be the happiest one of her life. She couldn't have been more thrilled wearing a new shirt from Neiman Marcus, than she was her old worn-out one with the cut-off tail.

A lot of small planes were flying in and out today, and she had plenty to do, filling tanks and checking oil. Best of all, most of the pilots noticed her missing shirttail and commented about it.

Pepper had just finished refueling a Seneca when she saw Kendall and Grant's Turbo Commander circle the airport and come in for a landing. Mr. Connolly, Greg's dad, would be flying it.

Standing by the gas pump, Pepper waited as he taxied the plane over and stopped.

"Hi, Pepper," he said as he stepped out the door. "How's it going?" He was a tall, well-built man with dark hair that was graying at the temples.

"Fine, Mr. Connolly."

"Greg tells me you're some student. Is he treating you okay?"

Pepper nodded, but didn't say anything because Mr. Kendall was climbing out of the plane. He was a distinguished-looking gentleman with silver hair and steel-gray eyes, and Pepper was slightly in awe of him.

"What's this?" he said, studying Pepper from beneath shaggy brows. "You mean we have a line girl now instead of a line boy?"

"That's right, Mr. Kendall. I'm taking over my brother's job."

"Think you could wash and wax this plane?"

"Sure," Pepper said. "I could be finished with it by Monday."

"Good. I have to go to Dallas Monday. If the plane looks okay, I'll have a two hundred dollar check for you."

"Don't worry. It will be ready," Pepper said confidently. For two hundred dollars, she would be crazy if it wasn't. Even though she knew that was the amount people paid to have a large plane washed and waxed, it still sounded like a gigantic sum of money. That would be a nice chunk to apply to her flying fund.

Mr. Kendall walked on out to his Mercedes and Mr. Connolly went into the lounge. When Pepper was finished refueling the plane, she went in to write up a ticket for the gas.

"Looks as if you soloed today," Greg's father said when she walked past him to go behind the counter.

Pepper nodded and smiled, but she didn't say anything. It would sound ridiculous for a beginner to talk about soloing to a pilot with thousands of hours.

"That's great," Mr. Connolly said. "It's an experience you'll never forget, no matter how many hours you log. I can still remember every detail of my solo in an old Aeronca Chief. Believe me, that's a lot different from flying a one fifty-two."

"I believe you, all right," Pepper said. "I probably wouldn't get to solo for another month if I had to do it in an Aeronca."

"Well, I imagine you're anxious to get busy washing the Commander. How would you like to taxi it? I'll sit in the co-pilot's seat."

"You mean it?" Pepper said, her eyes wide.

"I take it by that statement, you'd like to give it a try."

"Would I ever," Pepper said, happiness rippling through her. It was hard to believe so many nice things were happening in one day!

Since all of her work inside was finished, Pepper started washing the Turbo Commander as soon as they got it into position and Mr. Connolly left. It would take some hard work for the rest of today and all of Sunday afternoon if she were going to have it washed and waxed by Monday.

She was soon almost as wet as the plane, but she really didn't mind since it was such a hot afternoon. She was working on the wing when Greg walked around the corner of the building with Mr. Archer, his new student.

"Hi, Pepper," he said. "I see you found something to keep you busy."

Pepper groaned to herself. She had no idea Greg would be giving a lesson to anyone this afternoon. He always managed to see her when she looked the sloppiest. "This will keep me busy for quite a while," she said, and gave him a weak smile.

Bending her head, she started scrubbing furiously at the wing, and hoped Greg would go on without paying any attention to her bedraggled appearance. But why would he notice? she mused, as they walked on. After all, he was used to her this way—it was just a normal, everyday experience for him.

Greg and his student had been gone about a half an hour when Pepper had another visitor. The moment she glanced up and saw Stephanie, she felt like moaning again. Stephanie looked so cool, and lovely, and poised. She was wearing a dark blue sundress and white espadrilles, and her dark hair was tied back with a blue ribbon.

She walked over to the plane and stared up at Pepper with obvious astonishment. "Hi," she said. "Do you mean you *wash* planes, too?"

"That's right," Pepper said without enthusiasm.

"You're really amazing. I've never even washed my car except in a drive-through car wash."

Something about Stephanie rankled her, but Pepper couldn't decide what. She didn't act snobbish, but her cool, calm, collected manner still made Pepper feel inferior.

"Is there anything I can do for you?" Pepper asked.

"I need to talk with Greg," Stephanie told her. "Do you know where he is right now?"

"He went up with a student about half an hour ago. It may be quite a while before he's back."

"Oh, dear," Stephanie said, pushing out her lips.

"Can I give him a message for you?" Pepper asked, climbing down the stepladder.

"It's about our date this evening . . . let's see . . . I won't be at home, but I suppose I could leave a number where he can call me."

"Why don't you leave it by the schedule book on the counter in the lounge," Pepper suggested. "I'll tell Greg it's there."

"Okay, I will. Thanks a lot, Pepper," Stephanie said with a pleasant smile.

"Sure, any time," Pepper said. She tried to smile back, but her face felt stiff and unnatural.

After Stephanie left, Pepper leaned back against the

plane with a sigh and watched the orange and white Mooney 201 that was circling the airport. It would certainly help if Stephanie were a snob or maybe rude. At least then Pepper wouldn't feel so guilty about disliking her. She knew why she did, all right, but she hated to admit it even to herself. She was just plain jealous!

As the Mooney taxied up to the gas pump, Pepper stopped daydreaming and sprang into action. A middle-aged man stepped out of the pilot's side of the plane and a sharp-looking boy with blond hair climbed out the other door.

"I'm looking for Bill McNeil," the man said.

"His shop is on the other side of the big hangar," Pepper said. "Just go around the north side and in the first door."

Since the Mooney was a low wing, Pepper didn't have to bother with her stepladder.

The boy leaned against the side of the plane and smiled at her. "What's your name?" he asked.

"Pepper McNeil. What's yours?"

"Marty Owens. Dad and I have been to a lot of airports, but I've never seen such a pretty girl working at one before."

"Are you from around here?" Pepper asked, feeling slightly embarrassed.

"Oklahoma City, but we're on our way back from Little Rock. As long as we had to stop here anyway, my old man wanted to gas up. Big Horn has the cheapest gas around."

"You have a neat-looking plane," Pepper said.

"It flies like a dream," Marty said, running his hand through his wavy blond hair. "I'll have to buzz over and give you a ride someday."

"How long have you been a pilot?"

"Almost two years now. I got my license on my seventeenth birthday."

"That's exactly what I plan to do," Pepper said. She finished filling the last tank and they pulled the plane over and tied it down.

"Got anything to eat in there?" Marty asked, nodding toward the lounge.

"There are sandwich, chip, and pop machines."

"Why don't you sit down and drink a pop with me while I wait for my old man?"

When Marty called his father his "old man," it grated on Pepper's ears. She couldn't imagine calling her dad that even in his absence, but she knew a lot of kids did. Other than that, Marty seemed like an all right guy and it was nice after seeing Stephanie to have a boy even notice her as a girl.

"Sure, I'll drink a pop with you. I could use the break," Pepper said as they started walking toward the lounge.

Marty bought two pops, a sandwich and chips for himself, then came and sat down on the sofa opposite Pepper's chair.

"You look tired," he said, handing a pop to her. "What have you been doing?"

"Washing a Turbo Commander, and I've still got to wax it."

"You never did tell me what a pretty girl like you is doing working at an airport."

"Earning money for flying lessons. Besides, my folks are the managers."

"Boy, you must be crazy about flying. I'll *have* to take you for that ride someday."

"That's right," Pepper said with a laugh. "I'll be waiting." She wouldn't be holding her breath, though.

Somehow she had the feeling that Marty talked this way with every girl he saw.

At that moment the door opened and Mr. Archer walked in, followed by Greg. Greg looked from Marty to Pepper, then back to Marty again. It seemed to Pepper there was a flash of recognition between the two boys, but neither of them said anything.

"Pepper," Greg said in a gruff voice, "there's a plane waiting for you to refuel."

Greg certainly had his nerve. Who did he think he was, anyway? He'd never used that tone of voice with her before or told her how to do her work. Anger flashed through Pepper, and she bit her bottom lip hard to keep from smarting off to him. She would have said something if Mr. Archer and Marty weren't in the same room.

Pepper went to refuel the plane, but the more she thought about the way Greg had treated her, the more she fumed.

Just as she finished with the plane, Marty and his father walked out to theirs.

"I'll be seeing you, Pepper," Marty said with a wink and a wave.

Marty's words helped to soothe her damaged ego a little. At least *he* treated her decently. Pepper pulled the 172 into place and walked slowly back to the lounge. Maybe Greg would be gone and she wouldn't have to talk to him.

That wasn't the case, though. He was leaning against the counter talking on the phone when she came back in. From what he was saying, he must have found Stephanie's note and called her. She was glad in a way. At least it would give her a chance to get her things and leave.

Grabbing her logbook and computer off the counter, Pepper headed for the office.

"Just a minute, Pepper," Greg said, holding the phone with his hand over the mouthpiece. "I want to talk to you before you leave."

Pepper felt like sticking her nose up in the air and walking out, but she nodded and sat down to wait for him to finish. Evidently Greg realized how he had sounded and was going to apologize to her. Of course, she would accept. She couldn't stay angry with Greg even if she wanted to. She could feel the lump that squeezed in her throat melting away as she waited for his apology.

In fact, she almost felt happy again except for the fact that Greg was talking so sweetly to Stephanie. If only that were herself on the other end of the line instead.

"Okay, Stephanie," Greg said at last. "I'll be by at seven-thirty to get you."

Greg hung up the phone and turned to Pepper with a frown on his face. He studied her thoughtfully and Pepper felt as though his dark eyes were boring into hers.

"I'm really disappointed in you," Greg said slowly in the same gruff voice he had used with her previously.

"What are you talking about?" Pepper asked in surprise.

"You just don't seem like the kind of girl to flirt with every guy that flies in, especially when you have work to do."

"I . . . wasn't . . . flirting," Pepper sputtered. "Marty asked me to have a pop with him while he waited for his father."

"I still don't like it," Greg said, frowning even more. "He's not your type."

"How do you know?" Pepper asked. "This is the

first time you've ever seen him.'' She could feel her face flushing from anger and hurt at the same time.

"No it isn't. We had a class together once. Believe me, you and Marty aren't suited for each other and you'd better just steer clear of him.''

"Who appointed you my guardian?'' Pepper exclaimed. She couldn't believe he was acting this way.

"I appointed myself!'' Greg turned around and walked out the door, leaving Pepper with her mouth gaping open.

"Oh,'' Pepper said, stomping her foot, "I don't believe it!''

5

"Well, that looks like everything," Pepper said, standing back and surveying the picnic table on the patio. On one end sat the food: lemonade, chips, dip, and baked beans, and hamburgers and hot dogs ready to be grilled. At the other end were paper plates, plastic forks, napkins, and cups.

"It's a good thing you made that extra money washing Kendall and Grant's plane," Jeff said. "Otherwise we couldn't have afforded all this."

"That's right, and don't forget you still owe the money for your share," Pepper reminded him.

"How can I forget? You won't let me! At least I only asked you to chip in one-fourth of the expenses."

"Yeah, but you borrowed the other three-fourths from me."

Jeff laughed. "I'm lucky to have a rich sister." He walked over to the portable barbecue and dumped some charcoal in, then started the fire. "This ought to be just right by the time everyone gets here."

"Who all did you invite, anyway?"

"The guys Greg and I run around with. I told each of them to bring a date."

"Dates?" Pepper said, wrinkling her nose. "I didn't even think about that."

"I thought you understood what I was talking about when I told you to invite someone."

"You said to ask a friend," Pepper said in exasperation.

"Sorry, I didn't know I had to be so technical. Who'd you invite, anyway?"

"Linda."

"Did I hear my name mentioned?" Linda came walking around the corner of the house carrying her overnight bag, and stopped by the picnic table. "I came early to see if I could help, but it looks as if everything's ready."

"We'll be back in a little while," Pepper told Jeff as she and Linda went in the house.

"Jeff just told me that all of his friends are bringing dates," Pepper told Linda when they were in her room. "Guess you know where that leaves us."

"Probably stuck with all the work," Linda said with a laugh.

"Ugh," Pepper said, making a face. "I didn't even think about that. Well, at least we have paper plates and cups."

The girls checked their appearance in the full-length mirror on Pepper's door, then went out to the kitchen.

"Do you need any help?" Mrs. McNeil asked.

"All I have left to do is get the ice," Pepper said. She took the plastic bag out of the freezer and emptied the contents into a Styrofoam chest. "I'll bring you and Daddy a plate as soon as the first hamburgers are done."

"I hope that's soon. I'm making your father a sandwich right now to tide him over."

"I'll see if I can hurry the cook up," Pepper said with a laugh.

When Pepper and Linda went back out on the patio,

most of the guests had already arrived. Pepper used a pair of tongs to put ice in the cups, then Linda filled them with lemonade.

Just as they finished, Greg and Stephanie walked around the corner. Pepper almost dropped the cup of lemonade she was drinking. She hadn't even stopped to think that Greg would bring a date, too. And of course, it *would* have to be Stephanie!

She looked even prettier than usual, if that was possible. Although she wore a western outfit like everyone else present, somehow the clothing was transformed on her.

"Who's that?" Linda whispered.

"Stephanie Kendall." Pepper felt the muscles in her throat constricting and it seemed as if she were choking on the words.

Linda must have noticed because she looked at Pepper in a peculiar way. "Has Greg been dating her long?"

Pepper shrugged and tried to act nonchalant. "I don't think so. Jeff said they've only had a few dates."

Pepper tried to enjoy the barbecue, but her enthusiasm had completely drained away with Greg's and Stephanie's arrival. Wherever she looked during the evening it seemed she saw the two of them.

As soon as she could, after everyone finished eating, she went inside to clean up. In a short while Linda joined her.

"Okay," Linda said, joining Pepper at the sink, "You might as well tell me what's wrong. You've been moping around all evening."

"Have I really acted that bad?"

"Well, not quite, but you certainly aren't acting like yourself."

"I guess I'm still disgusted with Jeff for not telling me that everyone was supposed to bring a date," Pepper said. She stirred the dish suds with one hand and stared at it moodily. "You could have brought Jason if I had known."

"And who would you have asked?" Linda asked.

"Oh, uh . . . well . . . I don't know," Pepper stammered. "I haven't thought about it."

"Come on, Pepper," Linda coaxed. "You might as well tell me the truth. I wasn't born yesterday. Don't you think I can tell that you've got a crush on Greg?"

"How did you know?" Pepper asked in surprise, and wrinkled her brow in consternation. "You don't suppose anyone else noticed, do you?"

"No, but they don't know you as well as I do, either," Linda informed her.

"Well, it's hopeless, anyway," Pepper said, letting her shoulders sag. "I don't even want to think about it, let alone talk about it."

Linda brought the subject up again that night as they got ready for bed. "I don't know why you think the situation with Greg is hopeless. You said yourself he had only dated Stephanie a few times."

"Come on, Linda, you saw her. She's glamorous. Besides that, she's even nice."

"So what? You're pretty and nice, too."

"I appreciate the vote of confidence, but Greg just thinks of me as a sister. I don't know why he would ever feel differently with Stephanie around."

"Hold on a minute," Linda said, holding up her hand as if she were directing traffic. "Let's analyze this thing. Why does Greg think of you as a sister?"

"I suppose because he's known me since I was young."

"There's got to be more to it than that. Maybe he's used to seeing you in the same light, always doing the same thing and dressed the same way."

"You could be right," Pepper said slowly. "What do you suggest I do about it?"

"I hadn't actually figured anything out," Linda admitted.

"Oh, brother," Pepper said. "The way you started out, I thought you might have a manual at home with step-by-step instructions."

Linda laughed and shook her head. "If I did, it wouldn't work because whatever you do it has to be the real you, not just someone else's ideas."

During the remainder of the weekend, Pepper mulled over Linda's suggestions. She didn't intend to chase Greg, but why not let him see her in a new light? If only she could decide what that "new light" was going to be.

By Monday morning, Pepper had decided on the first step. She dressed for work in a pair of good jeans and western shirt as usual, but when it was almost time for her lesson, she changed into a dress she'd brought with her. After checking her appearance in the mirror, she ran a comb through her hair and applied a light touch of eye shadow and some lip gloss.

The results weren't bad, Pepper decided, and she certainly looked different from the way she usually did when Greg saw her. She felt different, too. Whirling around once, she watched her skirt billow out. Then she looked at her watch and rushed back out to the lounge.

Greg was already standing by the counter waiting for her. When she came in, he looked up and smiled.

"Hey," he said, "where are you going? I thought we had a flying lesson."

"We do," Pepper said, feeling terribly self-conscious. Her face grew hot and she was certain it must be the same color as her hair.

"Why are you all dressed up?"

This wasn't exactly the reaction she had hoped for, and Pepper's tongue felt tied in knots as she tried to explain. "I'm not dressed up. I'm . . . only . . . wearing a dress for a change. Some girls wear them all the time, you know."

"I'm just not used to seeing *you* in a dress," Greg said as they walked out to the plane.

"I wore them to school lots of times last year."

"Oh, I guess I never noticed," Greg said with a laugh. "Not that it matters, anyway."

Pepper felt like shaking Greg and telling him, Yes it does, it matters to me. Somehow this new image thing wasn't turning out at all as she had hoped.

By the end of the lesson, Pepper had forgotten all about her thwarted plans. Everything had gone great with her flying.

"You did a good job today," Greg said when they stopped at the gas pumps. "We'll start planning a cross-country. We'll try going Wednesday, so be thinking about where you'd like to go. Then Friday, you can do one on your own."

"Great, I can hardly wait!"

"Maybe you'd better not wear a dress, though," Greg said in a serious voice.

"Why not?" Pepper asked, knitting her brows.

"I wouldn't want anyone flirting with my good-looking student."

Though Greg said the words lightly, Pepper pondered

them for the remainder of the day. He didn't mean anything by what he said, she told herself one minute. Even Jeff occasionally said something just as nice when he wasn't teasing her. But the next moment she was wondering if Greg really thought she was nice-looking. Was he finally starting to notice her? What if he asked her for an honest-to-goodness date? According to Jeff, he and Stephanie weren't going steady.

Pepper's reveries were shattered by the conversation at the supper table that evening.

"We've got our plans all made for the trip next Saturday, Dad," Jeff said as he piled his plate high with mashed potatoes. "If all the girls' parents will let them go, we'll need to rent the two oh six."

"Where are you going?" Pepper asked.

"We're going to fly up to the Beaumont Hotel in Kansas and have dinner."

"Wish I could go sometime. I've heard it's a neat place."

"I wouldn't care if you came along, but we're going to be full up. I'm taking Janet, Bob and Debbie are going, and Greg's asking Stephanie."

"Oh," Pepper answered, nonplussed. *Greg and Stephanie* seemed to be a household phrase. She was beginning to wonder how many more times she could stand to hear it without screaming.

"Do you think all the girls' parents will let them go?" their mother asked.

"We've already promised to have them home by nine-thirty, so there shouldn't be any problem."

As their father cautioned Jeff about the flying, and their mother added an occasional comment, Pepper slowly ate her supper and tried to block out the whole discourse. Her efforts didn't work and she felt relieved when Jeff left for class. She might as well forget about Greg from now on, and just concentrate on her flying.

Too bad it wasn't that simple, she thought later as she lay in bed. She couldn't quit liking someone just because she decided to—especially someone as completely likable as Greg. She was glad she had her dual cross-country Wednesday and her solo one Friday to think about. Maybe that would take her mind off Greg for a little while.

That Friday, Pepper stood bent over the penciled figures on the flight log in front of her. With a pencil clamped between her teeth, she studied the calculations she had made for her cross-country.

"Are you sure forty-five hundred feet is the best altitude for the trip to Ardmore?" Greg asked.

"Well, the winds are better at nine thousand, but it would be silly to climb that high for such a short trip."

"Good thinking. I've seen people figure a cross-country using ridiculous altitudes with no consideration for what is practical," Greg said. "But of course I expected more of you. You're not stupid."

Pepper smiled with pleasure.

Greg scrawled an entry in Pepper's log book, snapped it shut, and gave her a big grin. "Okay, gal, your flight planning looks perfect and I've signed you off. Now, go show everyone in Ardmore and Central City what a fantastic pilot you are."

Pepper shot to attention, snapped her heels together, and brought her arm up in a crisp salute. "Aye, aye, captain," she said, smiling.

The morning sun had warmed the concrete and dried the dewy grass by the time Pepper's sandals clicked across the ramp toward the Cessna. Excitement quivered through her body. Today wouldn't be just a practice session flying around the airport doing landings or maneuvers.

Today Pepper would depart Big Horn airport for distant airports, flying over one hundred miles an hour high above the cultivated fields and rolling grasslands. Today was her day to find the pinpoint on the horizon that would be the airport where she would land. The day when she would stride from her plane at the Ardmore and Central City airports just as any other incoming pilot. And she knew that all those people that saw her would think of her only as the pilot that just flew in. Today was her day!

Scanning the sky for clouds, she surveyed the whole circle of blue around her. Only in the distant east could she detect the white cotton puffs above the hills. Her face broke into a smile once more. The weather was just as predicted.

After a thorough inspection of the plane, Pepper slipped behind the control wheel and clicked the seat belt and shoulder harness snugly into place.

"Clear," she shouted, alerting those within earshot that she was ready to start the engine.

She flicked the key and the engine churned to life. Her eyes immediately scanned the engine instruments, checking the oil pressure. Okay. The engine roared as she advanced the throttle and the plane pulled forward.

After taxiing to the end of the runway, Pepper meticulously ticked off the steps in the pretakeoff checklist. When all was in order, she taxied onto the runway and picked up the mike. "Cessna Four Seven Eight Two Romeo departing runway one seven Big Horn," she said in her most experienced-sounding voice.

Once again she advanced the throttle and with the

crescendo of the roaring engine, the plane accelerated down the runway.

She tugged lightly on the control wheel and she was airborne. Her eager craft soared skyward, leaving behind the curving roads, the stop signs, the traffic, the speed limits—every hindrance that earth travel imposed on man. She was free!

Ten miles southwest of Big Horn, Pepper's plane climbed steadily as it passed over her first checkpoint. The north edge of the lake was a dirty red contrasted to the lush greenness of the surrounding landscape. The sky's mellow blue added a cooling touch to the scene. Pepper gave a sigh, for as far as the eye could see the color of an Oklahoma summer exploded before her.

As the hands on the altimeter edged near 4500, she eased the nose of the plane over into level flight. As the airspeed increased, she slid back the throttle an inch and rolled the trim wheel until she could release the control wheel and the plane maintained its own level.

As the checkpoints slipped beneath the wings of her plane, Pepper jotted the time on the flight log. According to her calculations, she was on time and on course. But she wasn't surprised. "After all, I'm not stupid," she said to herself with a grin, thinking of Greg's words.

Pepper spotted the Ardmore airport fifteen miles out. At first it was only a bare spot scraped on the tree-strewn countryside. But as she drew closer she could see the three wide runways making a triangle on the ground. West of the runways was a row of buildings that had once been a military base but were now used for civil aviation. Southeast of the airport was the cluster of buildings and houses that made up the town of Ardmore.

"Ardmore Tower, this is Cessna Four Seven Eight Two Romeo ten miles north. Airport advisory, please," Pepper said into the plastic mike that touched her lips.

"Cessna Four Seven Eight Two Romeo, this is Ardmore Tower. The wind is out of the south, active runway is one seven, no reported traffic."

"Roger, and thank you," she said, then slid the mike back into its slot.

When Pepper swung the plane around to line up on final approach, she snapped down the flap switch and pitched the plane steeper. She watched with satisfaction as the ground rushed up to meet her, then stopped as she nosed the plane up in a flare. The tires gave a squeak as they whisked the concrete. She rolled down the runway and turned onto the taxiway toward the ramp.

Pepper parked in a spot on the ramp marked with a big yellow "T." After she shut the engine off, she swung her legs out the door of the plane and strode across the pavement to the flight office.

"Well, I'll say, they make pilots purdier and purdier every day," said a balding little man from behind a counter when Pepper walked in.

"Thank you," she said, giving the old fellow a prize-winning grin.

"Salty's my name, Salty Bohanan. And yours?" he asked with a chuckle.

"Well, I would laugh at your name, but mine is Pepper, Pepper McNeil." They both laughed.

"I reckon with names like ours we ought to get along just fine."

"I think so, Salty," Pepper said, finding she really liked the old man.

"What can I do for you, Pepper? Can I sell you some fuel?"

"No, I don't need fuel. Just need you to sign my log book."

"So you're a student pilot on your solo cross-country, are ya?"

"Yes, sir. I'm pretty excited about it, too," Pepper said, laying her log book on the counter.

Salty signed it and said, "I bet it's a whale of a day for flying," as he laid the book in her outstretched hand.

"It's beautiful up there," Pepper said, then, "Oh! I almost forgot. I've got to close my flight plan. Could I use your phone?"

"Sure, here, I'll dial the number for ya."

Pepper asked the flight station attendant to close her flight plan; then she filed one for the trip to Central City.

"Thanks, Salty. I would have been so embarrassed if the FAA had started a search for me."

"You wouldn't be the first," Salty said, smiling.

She knew she could end up talking to this charming old man all day if she didn't get going. With a promised return to Ardmore Municipal, she said good-bye and went out the screen door to the plane.

After another hour and another successful flight, Pepper was once again stepping out of the plane, this time at the Central City airport.

She had no sooner stepped into the airport lounge when she heard a familiar voice. "Well, would you look who came to see me?"

Pepper looked over to see Marty Owens sitting in one of the chairs, thumbing through a magazine.

"Oh, hi," she said, surprised and happy to see someone she knew.

"What are you doing here?" Marty asked as he stood and walked over to join her.

"I'm on my solo cross-country," Pepper answered, a feeling of pride welling up in her.

"I'm glad you remembered where I was from when you planned your trip."

"Actually, I didn't even think about it."

"Don't tell me that," Marty said, feigning a hurt look. "There I thought you'd come looking for me."

"Not hardly," Pepper answered with a laugh.

"Still, as long as you're here and we're old friends, you might as well let me buy you something at The Beacon."

"I could use something to drink," Pepper agreed. "Let me close out my flight plan and get my logbook signed first."

Marty nodded and walked with her to the counter. "Oh, yeah. We wouldn't want to forget one of their silly rules."

The man behind the counter studied Pepper as he signed her book. "So you're on your solo cross-country. We don't get many girls in here for that, especially as young as you are."

Pepper smiled her response. When the man was finished, she called in and closed her flight plan. Then she opened another one for the trip home, allowing forty-five minutes to spend on the ground.

"Well, that's taken care of," she said as she hung up the phone.

Marty placed a hand on her back and guided her

across the lounge to the small restaurant on the other side. "Sounded as if you're in a hurry," he said. "I was hoping you could spend a little more time with me."

"Not today," Pepper answered lightly.

"I hope that means some other time, then," Marty answered with a slow, crooked smile. "Now, what can I get you to drink? I'll go order from the counter. It's quicker."

"Whatever you're having," she said as she slid into a booth.

Marty returned in a short while with two large chocolate malts. "I thought maybe you'd like this. You don't look as if you need to watch your weight," he said as he sat down in the other booth.

"Thanks, it looks good."

"It's great that you happened to fly in today. I was just thinking about you."

"Oh, really?" Pepper asked, raising her eyebrow. She felt certain Marty was feeding her a line.

"Hey, I'm serious. I fell for you the first time I saw you." Reaching over, he laid his hand on top of hers. "You may not believe it, but just wait and see if I don't come and take you for that ride the first chance I get."

Pepper pulled her hand away and shrugged noncommittally. She wasn't sure she would want to go flying with Marty even if he really did come to take her.

6

"Are you absolutely sure that you're ready?" Greg asked for the third time as he and Pepper tied down the plane at Tulsa International Airport.

"Positive," Pepper answered. She couldn't keep from smiling at the expression on Greg's face. He was acting more nervous about her written exam than she was. "I don't know what you're worried about. It didn't bother you to solo me or send me on a cross-country."

"I knew you were ready those times, but you did this on your own."

"Wow, thanks a lot. I appreciate your support." Pepper tried to sound insulted, but she ended up laughing.

Greg looked down at her in surprise and then he laughed, too. "Sorry, I didn't realize how that would sound. Now don't forget—I'll meet you in the coffee shop at twelve o'clock, and don't worry. You'll do fine."

"Who's worried?" Pepper asked, grabbing her plotter and computer from the plane. Greg's obvious concern seemed to surround her with a warm, hazy glow, and she felt as if her feet weren't even touching the ground as she hurried to the General Aviation District Office.

In a short while, she was sitting in the test room with

four men and one woman who were already working on tests when she arrived. The room was completely silent except for the scratching of pencils and the hum of the electric clock on the wall.

Though all the questions covered material which she had studied thoroughly, the test was long and the problems took careful figuring. The only ones which really stumped her were a couple about weather. When she finished everything else, she worked on those two again. Then she went over every problem one more time and checked them for accuracy.

Exactly two and a half hours after she began, Pepper handed her test to the woman behind the counter.

"You'll receive your results in the mail in a week to ten days," the lady said with a pleasant smile.

After Pepper left the room, she strolled down the hall and looked in the coffee shop. It was only eleven-thirty and Greg wasn't there yet. Since she had no idea where he was, she sat down on a chair in the hall to wait for him. She was glad he had had business at the airport this morning, and had volunteered to come with her. She wouldn't have felt comfortable landing at such a big airport by herself, and driving seventy miles one way would have been worse. As it was, they got everything taken care of at once, and she even got to take a lesson on the way.

With a sigh, Pepper leaned her head back against the wall and closed her eyes. It was nice to have her written test out of the way, and she felt confident that she had done a good job. Wouldn't it be neat if she made a 100? She'd never heard of anyone doing that, but it would be fun to see Greg's reaction if she did. He might even hug her again.

"What time did you get finished?" Greg's voice

71

interrupted Pepper's musings and she looked up to see him standing in front of her.

"Eleven-thirty."

"Did you check over all your answers?"

"Every one." She stood and they walked into the coffee shop.

"Any trouble?" Greg asked, his mouth set in a firm, straight line.

"There were a couple of weather questions that threw me," Pepper admitted as they sat down at a corner table. "What's Virga?"

"That's a wisp or streak of precipitation that evaporates before reaching the ground."

"Wouldn't you know," she said with a moan. "There goes my score of one hundred. Did you ever think you'd get one hundred?"

"I plan to every time I take a written test, but I've never made it above ninety-six."

"I think it's good to set a goal high to begin with," Pepper said after the waitress came and took their order.

"I agree," Greg said. "It's kind of like the old saying about reaching for the stars."

"Exactly, or chasing the sun. I suppose it sounds silly, but that's how I feel sometimes when I'm flying— kind of like I'm doing something that really isn't possible."

"I know exactly what you mean," Greg said.

When he smiled a slow, warm smile at her that lit up his dark eyes and crinkled them at the edges, Pepper felt a deep understanding flow between them. It was an affinity which she knew Greg felt, too, as his eyes held hers for a long, spellbinding moment. Then the waitress appeared with their sandwiches and the spell was broken.

That night as she lay in bed, Pepper's thoughts kept

returning to that brief interlude in the coffee shop. Though nothing had really happened, at the same time something momentous had occurred.

She thought fleetingly about Marty, too. He was nice-looking and fun, but he just wasn't the same caliber person that Greg was. She'd choose Greg over any guy, any day. Now what he needed was an opportunity to feel the same way about her. How he would ever get that chance might be quite a problem, Pepper reflected as she drifted off to sleep.

Friday evening at supper, Jeff unwittingly supplied the answer to her dilemma.

"You got any plans for tomorrow night?" he asked.

"Nope."

"That's good. Stephanie canceled out for the trip up to Beaumont Hotel. I told Greg maybe you could come along since it's kind of short notice to ask another girl. You want to go?"

Pepper almost choked on her green beans. "Well . . . uh . . . sure, I guess I can," she stammered, "if Dad and Mom don't care." The very thing she had dreamed about! She felt as if Jeff had handed her a gift on a silver platter.

"I don't know who would take better care of you than your own brother and Greg," Mr. McNeil said.

"Sounds like the perfect solution to me," Mrs. McNeil said.

Pepper could feel her cheeks flaming from embarrassment. Bending her head so no one would notice, she traced a pattern on the checkered placemat with the handle of her fork. "What are the other girls wearing?" she asked in a raspy voice.

"It's not that fancy a place, but they're going to dress

up. Don't let that scare you off, though. Any of your church dresses would be okay.''

"No problem," Pepper said, shrugging her shoulders matter-of-factly, but it was all she could do to contain her excitement. What, oh what could she wear? she wondered desperately. The few nice dresses she had didn't seem right for the occasion.

As soon as everyone had finished eating, Pepper rushed through the after-supper clean-up. Then she went to her room and started digging through her closet. When every dress she owned was lying on the bed, she plopped down in her desk chair. Propping her elbows on her knees and her chin in her hands, she stared at the sparse selection.

She chewed on her bottom lip and shook her head slowly. None of them was right, but with all the expense of her flying lessons, she just couldn't afford to buy a new dress.

Pepper heard a tap on the door and glanced up as her mother walked in. Her mom looked at the dresses, then back to Pepper. Clearing a corner on the end of the bed, she sat down and faced Pepper. "Nothing to wear tomorrow evening?"

"Not really, but I guess it doesn't matter."

"I think it means a lot to you," her mother said softly, and Pepper shifted uncomfortably under her mom's careful scrutiny. "Since tomorrow is one of the Saturdays you don't work, I thought you might like to go shopping."

"I already thought about that, but I can't even afford to buy a new purse right now, let alone a new dress."

"I didn't say anything about you buying a dress. *I'll* buy it and we'll even have lunch someplace. How does that sound?"

"Wonderful, Mom. Thanks!"

"There is a new shop that I was in the other day called The Rose Garden. It has some nice things and the prices are reasonable."

"I don't care where we go. Any place will be great."

"It's a date, then," her mother said, rising to leave.

"Thanks again, Mom," Pepper said, coming over and hugging her tightly. "You're super!"

"You're pretty super yourself."

The following morning, they left early so they could be at the shop when it opened. "We want to have plenty of time to look somewhere else if necessary," her mother said as they climbed into the green Toyota.

"That's right, we don't have all day. But what if I can't find anything?" Pepper asked in a sudden panic. "I don't know what I'll wear then."

"Don't worry. We'll find just the thing," her mother assured her as she backed the car out the drive and onto the blacktop road leading to the highway.

"I hope so."

Fifteen minutes later, they were looking through the rack of Junior dresses at The Rose Garden. Pepper had chosen four other dresses to try on when she spotted *the* dress. It was the color of a new leaf, and made of a semi-sheer voile.

Her mother noticed it at the same time. "Now that is made for you," she said.

"It's beautiful, but too elegant for where we're going."

"Bring it along, anyway. You've got to at least try it."

The owner of the store ushered them to the spacious dressing room. "If you find something you really like," she told them, "come out and look in the mirror in the shop. The lighting is much better out there."

Pepper hung *the* dress, as she thought of it, behind the others. "I'll save that for dessert," she said, flashing her mother a smile.

After trying on the other three dresses, she decided on a blue cotton sundress with a linen jacket. "It's perfect for this evening," she said, admiring the way the full skirt accented her small waist.

"There's still the green one," her mother reminded her.

"I almost hate to try it on," Pepper admitted. "I'm going to love it and I don't want to."

"Why not?" her mom asked as she helped Pepper take off the sundress and slip the green one over her head.

"I wouldn't have anyplace to wear it."

"You never know. It's always good to be prepared, and besides, it's the type of dress you can wear year round." Her mother zipped up the back and turned her around to face the mirror.

Pepper stared into the wide eyes of a beautiful girl she scarcely recognized. The medium shade of green was perfect, making her eyes appear the color of jade. The wide lace edging the long sleeves and neck gave her an almost Victorian look, and yet the V neckline was slightly sexy at the same time.

"I love it," she said in a breathless voice.

"So do I. We'll get both," her mother said decisively.

After putting the dresses in the car, they walked a block and a half to a chic little restaurant called Le Café. It was one of her and her mother's favorite places to go on the few occasions when they went to lunch together. Pepper enjoyed the quiet atmosphere and the candles glowing softly on the table.

After ordering a chicken crepe with mushrooms, Pepper leaned across the table and whispered to her mother. "Thanks again for the new dresses and for lunch. I really appreciate your doing all this for me."

"I'm glad you're pleased, dear. You'll look pretty this evening, and I hope you have a nice time."

"I do, too. I only wish we were going someplace where I could wear the green dress. Then maybe . . ." Realizing what she had almost said, Pepper clamped her lips tightly together and searched unsuccessfully for an appropriate ending to the sentence. She couldn't just tell her mother how badly she wanted Greg to see her in the green dress.

"Looking glamorous never hurt anyone's chances with a boy, but you look lovely in your blue sundress, too." A smile played around the corner of her mother's mouth as she added, "A boy like Greg would consider more than surface appearance and you're a beautiful person inside as well."

"Spoken like a true mother," Pepper said with a little laugh. She just couldn't look her mom in the eye, so instead stared down at the napkin that she was nervously twisting.

She should have realized her mother would guess how she felt about Greg. She had always been able to read Pepper's thoughts. But as much as she would like to talk over the whole situation with her mom, she couldn't bring herself to say another word. If she mentioned anything remotely connected with Greg, she knew her voice would squeak.

Her mother seemed to sense her discomfort and changed the subject. After that, they chatted away about nothing during the leisurely lunch.

On the short trip back, Pepper leaned her head back against the seat, closed her eyes, and dreamed about her date that evening. She hoped Greg would have a nice time. Maybe he would enjoy her company so much that he would even kiss her good night! Not very likely since it wasn't really a date, she reminded herself. She was merely filling in for Stephanie, and then only because her brother suggested the idea. Still, it would give Greg the opportunity to notice she was a real live girl.

As soon as they got home, Pepper took her new dresses to her room, then went to the bathroom to take a bath. She wanted to be out of Jeff's way so he could get ready after work. Sometimes she wondered if it wouldn't be easier to share a bathroom with a sister than a brother. Probably not, according to the tales she'd heard from friends who had sisters.

Using the stepstool, she reached for the bottle of bubble bath on the top shelf. Her Aunt Delphi gave her a bottle every Christmas, and Pepper usually gave it to her mom or Linda. This time she'd stuck it in the cabinet. After pouring a few capfuls under the running water, she watched as mountains of suds appeared. The stuff was definitely bubbly.

After soaking in the tub for a half hour, Pepper shampooed her hair. Back in her room once more, she blow-dried it and then decided to use the curling iron. *I should do this more often,* she thought as she admired her reflection in the mirror. The curling iron had added just the right amount of softness to her hair.

Dressed at last in the blue sundress, she felt pleased with the results. When she went out to the kitchen to wait for Jeff, her mother looked up from the carrots she was peeling and smiled her approval.

"You look lovely, honey. I don't see how *any* boy could resist you."

"You're just prejudiced, Mom. But I hope you're

right," she added softly as butterflies fluttered around her stomach.

When Jeff came out to the kitchen a short while later, he cast a brief glance in Pepper's direction, then stuck his head around the corner and looked in the dining room. "Excuse me," he said, turning back to them and clearing his throat. "I was looking for my sister, but I can't seem to find her."

"Very funny," Pepper said, pulling a face. "You have seen me in a dress before, you know."

"Maybe so, but you've never looked this good. It's hard to believe you're the same little girl who works at the Big Horn airport."

"Flattery will get you anywhere, but if you're wanting to borrow some money, I don't have any."

"Believe it or not, this is a genuine compliment."

"In that case, thanks. You look pretty good yourself," Pepper said, smiling at her tall, handsome brother.

"I'm going out to preflight the plane. You might as well come along now," he said. "Everybody's meeting out there."

"Aren't you going to get Janet?"

"Greg's bringing her for me since she lives right on his way. By the way, he and I are going to fly on the trip over, but you can get some night flying in with Greg on the way back."

"That's fine with me," Pepper said, feeling happy that she got to sit by Greg at all even if it was at the controls of the plane.

Just as Jeff finished preflighting the plane, Greg came with Janet and a short while later, Bob and Debbie arrived. At exactly five o'clock, the 206 took off for Beaumont.

The evening was still, and the flight a pleasant one. If

Pepper had to sit by anyone other than Greg, she was glad it was Janet. The petite brunette had been Jeff's steady girlfriend for a year, and Pepper really liked her.

Beaumont, Kansas, didn't look like much from the air when they spotted it about forty-five minutes after they left Big Horn. It consisted of a few houses, the hotel, and a wooden water tower.

"This is your captain speaking," Greg said loudly as Jeff circled the grass strip. "If you will look out your windows to the right, you will notice an historical point of interest. Situated next to the railroad tracks is the only operational wooden water tower in the United States."

Jeff brought the plane down gently, and in a few moments they were taxiing toward the street that led to the hotel. Then, instead of stopping, he taxied right out onto one of the two main streets in the town and continued until he came to the four-way stop sign.

Pepper smiled to herself, knowing what the others were thinking as they stared at each other in stunned disbelief.

"Jeff!" Janet wailed. "Can't you get in trouble for this?"

After looking both directions, he taxied the plane across the intersection.

"I forgot to explain," Greg said, leaning around his seat with a mischievous grin. "This is also probably the only town in the U.S. where it's legal to taxi a plane on the street."

Bob, Debbie, and Janet let out signs at the same time and then they all started laughing.

"Next time I go anywhere with you, Jeff McNeill, I want a complete briefing on the flight first," Janet said as Jeff parked the plane by the hotel.

After everyone climbed out of the plane, Greg came around and walked by Pepper's side to the hotel. It was an old two-story structure built almost a hundred years ago but kept in good condition, and renowned among pilots for its good food.

Once inside the restaurant, the group chose a table by the window.

They all seemed to enjoy themselves, but Pepper found herself wishing that she and Greg could be here alone. He was nice and friendly as usual, but he was just as friendly with Janet and Debbie as he was with her.

After dinner, everyone decided to explore the town and meet back at the plane at seven forty-five. Jeff and Janet left first, then Bob and Debbie. Pepper felt vaguely uncomfortable sitting at the table alone with Greg. If only she could read his mind. Was he thinking about Stephanie and wishing he hadn't got stuck with Pepper?

"Well, what do you want to do?" Greg asked. "Would you like to take a closer look at that old water tower?"

"That sounds fine."

Greg walked around to her chair and pulled it out for her. "Let's go then."

The water tower was right across the street from the hotel. When they reached it, Greg stood back and read the sign attached to one of the wooden legs: "Original Frisco Watertower. Last remaining operating wooden watertower in the United States." Using the same leg as a support, he leaned back and smiled at Pepper, then gazed out at the surrounding countryside.

"This is a pretty evening for flying," Pepper said, leaning against one of the other legs.

"It really is, and speaking of pretty, I forgot to tell you how nice you look this evening."

"Thank you," Pepper murmured. She could feel herself blushing and didn't look at Greg as she spoke.

"I'm glad you got to come, but I want you back home and to bed early. You need your rest for that next cross-country tomorrow. Why don't we go sit on the lounge chairs in front of the hotel and wait for the others?" Greg said. "There are a few points I want to go over with you about it."

It was hopeless, Pepper realized with a sinking feeling in the middle of her stomach. Somehow the conversation always managed to get back to flying. And it would have to be right when she thought it was headed in a different direction.

In fifteen minutes the others were back and soon they were swishing across the grass of the darkening runway, heading for home.

"Level off at fifty-five hundred," Greg said. He had turned the controls over to Pepper shortly after takeoff. This was to be her first experience piloting a plane at night.

After they leveled out, Greg adjusted the power, prop, and mixture controls. The steady drone of the engine was the only sound heard in the airplane. Everyone seemed lost in the bliss of night settling over the land. The smear of red on the horizon faded fast, leaving them wrapped in a dark blanket pierced with tiny pinholes of light where stars above, and ranchers' arc lamps below, shown through.

"It's so beautiful, Greg," Pepper said with a sigh.

"I know. It's always a thrill for me to fly on nights as perfect as this. I don't think I'll ever tire of it."

The lights of a large town seemed to slide toward them, drawing closer.

"That must be Bartlesville up ahead. I can tell by the

way the town seems split in two and the airport beacon is north of the west part of town.''

"That's right. Can you see Tulsa?''

"Well, no. I think we're too far away, aren't we?''

"Look on the horizon ahead and a little to the left. Do you see that glow?''

"Yes. But . . .''

"That's Tulsa. It's just over the horizon from us and all you can see of it is the lights shining on the clouds above. Once you orient yourself at night, it's hard to get lost.''

Once again the droning engine was all that broke the silence. It seemed they were sitting in a theater box above the world, watching it spin beneath them, the night was that calm. It was a time for being silent. And it stayed that way for most of the flight home except when Greg gave her a few words of instruction.

"Right on time,'' Jeff said when they landed at the Big Horn airport. "We've got just enough time to get you girls home, and that should convince your parents to let you do this again.''

"You guys go on,'' Greg said. "I'll take care of the plane and put it in the hangar.''

"Do you want me to help?'' Pepper asked after the others left.

"Nope.''

"Okay, then,'' Pepper said, the words seeming to stick in her throat.

"You're too pretty to mess with gassing an airplane tonight,'' Greg said as he pulled the gas nozzle over to the plane, "but why don't you wait for me and I'll walk you home?''

"All right.''

After Greg finished gassing the plane, they taxied it over to the hangar and Pepper helped tie it down.

"Ready to go?" Greg asked, holding out his hand to her when they were finished.

Nodding, she gave him her hand and they walked out the wide door together. To her surprise, Greg continued to hold her hand as they strolled toward the house.

When they stopped at the door, Pepper took a deep breath. "I had a nice time," she said in a quavery voice.

"So did I," Greg said. He smiled down at her and Pepper knew he was going to kiss her. As he leaned lower, she shut her eyes in breathless anticipation.

"Thanks for going with me, kiddo," he whispered in her ear, then tweaked her on the cheek.

7

"Did you have a nice time, honey?" Pepper's mother asked as soon as she came through the door.

"Oh, sure . . . just great. Beaumont's a real nice place," she said. Her parents were sitting together on the sofa listening to their collection of Big Band records from the fifties. They were holding hands and her mother's head was resting on her dad's shoulder.

"Sit down and tell us about it," her father invited.

"I . . . uh . . . have kind of a headache. Thought I'd go on to bed. Good night," she said as she made a hasty retreat.

Ordinarily Pepper was happy that she had parents who showed affection in front of their children, but she didn't want to sit in the living room with them tonight and see them snuggled up together on the sofa. It was more than she could bear.

Jeff was probably kissing Janet good night right now, and Bob kissing Debbie. Pepper felt completely left out and alone. If she hadn't been so certain that Greg was about to kiss her good night, she probably wouldn't be so disappointed.

They did have a nice time though, she had to admit, and he even mentioned twice how nice she looked. Then when he held her hand on the way home, that clinched everything. She was sure at the time that he actually liked her as a girl instead of as his best friend's sister.

Pepper pursed her lips as she got ready for bed and climbed in. She was going to have to quit assuming things. Greg might have held her hand because he did think of her as a kid sister. He probably felt some sort of misguided responsibility about seeing her home safely.

Rolling to her stomach, she punched the pillow and tried to think of something else. Maybe he did like her, but he thought it was too soon for a kiss. If that was the case, though, he wouldn't have called her "kiddo." But then, he might not realize that she liked him. So what could she do about it? She had no intention of chasing any boy, even if he was the most handsome and wonderful guy in the whole world.

His image was as clear in her mind as if it were a photograph—the smooth sheen of his brown hair, the confident way he held his broad shoulders. His dark eyes were usually filled with laughter, except for the few times she had seen him angry, like when he had scolded her about Marty Owens. Then his eyes seemed to shoot sparks. What would it be like to have his strong, tanned arms hold her close, to feel his lips on hers?

She had to stop this and get some rest, Pepper told herself. But the harder she struggled to go to sleep, the more wide awake she became. She heard the crunch of gravel in the drive when Jeff came home, and the murmur of voices from the living room.

Eventually everyone went to bed and the house became quiet, but still she lay wide-eyed, staring into her softly moonlit room. The airport's rotating beacon usually gave her a safe feeling, but tonight it was one more thing to keep her awake.

Finally she could stand it no longer. She had to do something! Throwing back the covers, she climbed out of bed and walked stealthily across the room. Without turning on a light, she got dressed, then opened her door quietly and tiptoed down the hall, through the living room, and out the front door.

Once outside, Pepper drew in a deep breath of the softly scented night air. What she needed was some good hard work to wear her out and take her mind off Greg. With a slight toss of her head, she squared her shoulders and strode purposefully toward the airplanes that were tied down by the main hangar.

She might as well wash Romeo, the plane she was using for her cross-country tomorrow afternoon. In a few moments she had it untied and attached the tow bar. If only her Romeo would pay some attention to her, she thought woefully as she turned on the water full force and sprayed the plane. A good amount of the water splashed back on her and she shivered slightly.

Pepper scrubbed at the plane for about fifteen minutes, but the vigorous activity did nothing to loosen the knot of pain in her chest.

"Just where I thought I might find you!"

Her mother's voice surprised Pepper and she jumped.

"You scared me. I didn't hear you coming."

"Anyone could have sneaked up on you," her mother admonished her. "I don't like you out here by yourself at night." Walking over to Pepper, she put her arm around her shoulder. "Did you have that bad a time tonight, honey?"

Pepper shrugged and rubbed the toe of one tennis shoe against the concrete. "No . . . it was fine . . . I guess I'm kind of mixed up about some things . . . and I couldn't sleep."

"Would it help to talk about them?" Picking up a rag out of the bucket of soapy water, her mother started scrubbing the plane where Pepper had left off.

"I don't know, it's just that——"

"Just that you really like Greg and you don't know whether the feeling is mutual?"

"Exactly," Pepper said. There was a funny catch in her throat and she didn't know if she would be able to discuss anything about Greg with her mother. She began washing the plane again.

"Greg has known you since you were a young girl. I think he does like you, but he needs some time to see you in this new perspective."

"But there's Stephanie," Pepper said as she walked around to the other side of the plane. "She's gorgeous and even kind of nice. I can't begin to compare with her."

"You don't have to. The best thing you can do is be your own exuberant self. From what I've heard, Greg isn't going steady with Stephanie. You and he have so many things in common and that counts for a lot."

There was really no argument against her mother's philosophy, she thought as they finished the plane together. She only hoped her mom was right.

"Thanks for helping me with the plane," Pepper said when they at last walked back to the house.

"You're welcome, but no more of this plane washing at night. Do you understand? I don't want you out by yourself and I'm too old for that kind of thing," her mother said with a laugh.

"All right. Thanks for—for the encouragement, too," Pepper said when they were at the door.

"Sure, honey, and I was being honest when I said I believe Greg likes you. Remember, I've known him for a long time. Just give him a while. I think he's still a little surprised at his own feelings."

"What else can I do *but* wait?" Pepper said, heaving her shoulders.

"Go to bed, for one thing. And try to get some sleep!"

"Okay."

She'd try, but she didn't know if it would do any good. If there was one thing she had learned, it was that she couldn't shut off thoughts of Greg just because she wanted to. She would probably stay awake all night thinking about him, she reflected as she climbed into bed once more. Obviously, her heart couldn't be ruled by her head.

If only, if only her mother were right, Pepper thought as she drifted to sleep with the image of a tall brown-haired boy with dark eyes and a captivating smile.

Maybe her mom did know what she was talking about, Pepper decided early the next afternoon as she and Greg discussed her flight plan for her cross-country.

"Everything looks fine," Greg said. "How long did you estimate this trip would take you?"

"It's about two hours and fifteen minutes in the air, so with the two stops—I'd say no longer than three hours altogether."

"Have you checked weather?" Greg asked.

"The man at Flight Service said it was going to be beautiful," she said with a grin. "He even said he wished he could go along."

Greg's eyes twinkled in a smile, then he sobered. "Is that all he said?"

"Well, he did say there was a chance of some cloud build-ups to the west late tonight. But that won't be a problem for my flight."

"Probably not, but on warm, humid days things can happen fast with the weather. I'm sure your flight will be fine, but if things start looking bad, don't take any chances. Land at the nearest airport and call me collect."

Cocking her head, Pepper studied him for a moment. "You knew what the weather was supposed to be like, didn't you?"

"I wouldn't send someone out without personally checking the weather," Greg said. "Especially you. I can't let anything happen to my best student," he added, patting her arm.

Greg's touch sent a warm thrill through Pepper and she felt almost dizzy from the emotions churning inside of her.

"I'll be here with another student when you get back, and I'll be anxious to hear all about your trip."

"Okay. I guess I'd better get going."

Pepper thought about the sincere look in Greg's eyes as she walked out to the plane and preflighted. She felt certain that he didn't show so much care for his other students.

Once again the exhilaration of solo flight thrilled her as she soared upward. Thoughts of her freedom in the air, the beauty of the summer day, and Greg kept her smiling all the way to McAlester.

At the north end of town, Pepper shuddered as she looked down on the ominous high-walled compound of the state penitentiary. It didn't seem possible at that moment that there were people in the world who did wrong. She shrugged off the thought and prepared to land at the airport on the southern edge of town.

Pepper circled the airport and slid in for a perfect landing on runway one nine. After stopping long enough for the line boy to sign her logbook, she was off again, heading for Muskogee.

The airport at Muskogee was an old military base turned over to the city. The runway was so big she could have landed five times without having to circle. It seemed as if she taxied two miles getting to the ramp. Pepper could visualize big Air Force jets parked all over the base.

It must be exciting to be an Air Force pilot, she thought to herself. But there were no jets and hardly any planes. The old base was like a ghost town. Besides the half dozen planes parked on the ramp, the only things with wings were the starlings making nests wherever they could and two four-engined relics she thought must be Constellations.

When her logbook was signed, Pepper climbed into her plane and once again zipped down the runway and sailed into the summer sky. She smiled. She liked the airport people and pilots. Then suddenly she laughed. You silly girl, she thought. Of course you like airport people. That's what you have been since you were born.

Ten miles from Big Horn, Pepper picked up the mike. "Big Horn UNICOM, this is Cessna Four Seven Eight Two Romeo, airport advisory, over."

"Cessna Four Seven Eight Two Romeo, this is Big Horn UNICOM. The wind is out of the south, we're using runway one seven, no reported traffic. How was the trip, Pepper?" She recognized her mother's voice.

"Great, Mom. See you in a minute." As Pepper approached the airport she saw a touch of dark clouds building on the western horizon. Just as the weather man predicted, she thought. No problem with weather. Her flight had been perfect. But she was glad there had been a chance of thunderstorms. Otherwise Greg wouldn't have had an opportunity to show his concern for her.

The wheels squeaked on the runway and Pepper was home.

After Pepper refueled the 152 and tied it down, she practically bounded into the lounge. She could hardly wait to go over her trip with Greg! Her heart was already doing acrobatics at the prospect of spending some more time with him. She knew she hadn't just imagined the concern in his voice or the caring look in his eyes.

"Hi, Mom," she said enthusiastically. "Where's Greg?"

"He's up with a student. He said if you got back before he did, to tell you to stick around."

Pepper felt surrounded by a glow of happiness. "He said he wanted to hear all about my flight when I got back," she explained to her mother.

"That sounds like a good sign to me," her mother said, smiling.

"Things do look more promising to me today than they did last night."

"I'm glad. You know the old saying—'It's always darkest before the dawn.' Now, I'm sure you won't mind if I go on home. See you later, hon." She reached out and ruffled Pepper's hair as she walked by. "Have a nice time."

How could she help but have a nice time? Pepper asked herself as she watched her mother walk out the door. Wasn't she going to be with Greg? What more could a girl want?

She felt as if she were still up in the air as she went

back outside. Sitting down in one of the metal lawn chairs, she scanned the sky for any sign of an airplane. It was a sultry afternoon and the air felt thick and heavy. If she weren't watching for Greg, she would have gone back inside the air-conditioned coolness of the building.

After about fifteen minutes she spotted 741 Juliet, the other 152 from the flight school, approaching from the east. That would be Greg and his student, she thought happily as it circled the airport and landed. In a little while they would be laughing and talking about her trip, and maybe he would gaze at her with that special look which seemed to hold a promise for the future.

Pepper met the plane at the gas pump. "I'll gas up for you," she told Greg as he and his student climbed out.

"I hate to make you work on your day off, but thanks. I appreciate it," Greg said. "How'd everything go?"

"Just great.

"That's good. I'll be back in a minute."

Pepper smiled to herself as she watched Greg and his student walk to the lounge. Greg seemed to be in a hurry, but she knew he would be different when he came back alone.

He returned in a few moments, glancing down at the watch on his tan arm as he strode over to where she was standing. At the same instant, she noticed Stephanie drive up in her blue Corvette. A cold feeling began in Pepper's stomach and seemed to spread out over her entire body, even as she wiped the beads of perspiration from her forehead with the back of her hand.

"I didn't mean for this lesson to take quite so long," Greg said. "Thought I'd have some time for you to brief me on your trip, but we've got plans for this evening and I've got to go. You can tell me about everything tomorrow, okay?''

Pepper heard Greg's voice as if from a great distance. He was waiting for an answer, she realized. Without meeting his eyes, she nodded her head and busied herself with the plane.

She could hear the faint scraping sound of his shoes on the concrete as he walked away, but she didn't turn her head to look. Catching her bottom lip between her teeth, she reached up to brush away a tear.

8

Pepper had no idea how long she stood rooted to the concrete, staring out at the criss-cross pattern of the runways. She might have stayed there forever if another plane hadn't circled the airport with the intention of landing.

The plane wasn't one that was kept at Big Horn, but it seemed vaguely familiar. She recognized the red-orange Mooney 201 from somewhere. Dashing inside to the lounge, Pepper splashed some cool water on her face from the water fountain. She wouldn't want anyone to think she had been crying.

When she came outside again, Marty Owens was climbing out of the door of the plane. He waved and Pepper waved back.

He walked over to where she was standing. "I was hoping I'd find you here today," he said, cocking an eyebrow and smiling with self-assurance. "I've come to take you for that ride. Can you go now?"

"I suppose I can," Pepper said a little uncertainly. "I'll have to tie down that plane first," she said, pointing at the 152 still parked by the gas pump.

"I'll help you," Marty offered.

He was acting more decent than Greg, Pepper thought with a burst of righteous indignation. After Greg's commiserative remark about hating to have her refuel the plane on her day off, he had left it for her to put away! Suddenly the idea of going for a flight with Marty seemed like exactly what she wanted to do.

After moving the plane and tying it down, Pepper called her mother on the intercom to tell her she was going flying with a friend.

Pepper put the receiver in place and turned to Marty. "All ready," she announced.

"Great, you're really going to like this plane. It will make the bird you've been flying seem like a tricycle."

Pepper followed Marty to the Mooney and buckled herself in beside him.

"Aren't you going to preflight the plane, Marty?" Pepper asked.

"I checked it before I left Central City. Besides, I know this plane like the back of my hand. Don't worry, it's not going to fall apart," he said with a laugh.

As they taxied out to the runway, Pepper noticed another plane in the traffic pattern. It was turning on to final approach. She was puzzled why Marty hadn't turned on the radios. Greg had always insisted that she have the one in the 152 on to listen for approaching planes. As they reached the run-up area, Pepper relaxed in expectation of the routine engine run-up. But to her amazement, Marty pulled the Mooney onto the runway not only without a run-up, but without looking.

"Marty, look out, that other plane . . ." she screamed. Before Marty could respond, the other plane zoomed overhead with a roar and climbed away, going around for another try at a landing.

"Crazy guy," Marty said in anger.

"What do you mean, 'crazy guy'? You pulled out in front of him," Pepper said in trembling disbelief.

"Yeah, I guess it wasn't his fault. Oh well, no harm done. He'll make it the next time." He laughed again as he pushed the throttle forward and the plane accelerated down the concrete.

It wasn't the smoothest of takeoffs. Marty seemed to jerk the plane into the air and it bobbled with one wing dipping down perilously low to the ground. At first she thought he had forgotten how to fly. But then she noticed the flapping wind sock as they went by it and felt the bumpiness in the air. The wind was beginning to pick up.

They were climbing through two thousand feet when Marty looked over at Pepper. "It should be climbing better than this," he said with a worried look on his face.

Pepper glanced down to see a green landing gear light shining on the dash. "Why don't you retract the landing gear?" she asked, not knowing whether to smile or be afraid of this sloppy pilot.

"Oh, yeah," he said with a tinge of redness flushing his cheeks. He reached down and pulled the gear lever into the up position. The green light blinked off and she felt a bump as the gear tucked itself away in the belly of the plane.

They were soon leveled out and winging their way between billowy puffs of clouds that had suddenly appeared from nowhere.

"That was a close call back there with that other plane," Pepper said.

"Yeah, I guess so. I'll have to look for other planes next time," he said with a shrug.

"I thought you were going to run-up the engine or I would have told you about that other plane. How come you didn't?"

97

"Like I said, I know this plane like the back of my hand. My dad keeps it in top shape."

Pepper had been in aviation since she was born and she had never heard or seen anyone so flippant about flying. She didn't like it.

"You're making me scared, Marty. I want to go back. Besides, the weather is getting bad. Look at the clouds. They're getting thicker and blacker," she said looking around her and seeing the danger for the first time.

"Oh, don't worry," Marty said in a sing-song voice as if he were putting up with a whining child. "We'll be all right. This plane can do a whole lot more than that kite you're used to. Just relax and leave it to ol' Marty."

Leaving it to "ol' Marty" was the last thing that would make her relax. Pepper knew what bad weather was and she was looking at it out of her window at that moment. Marty was flying into the worst part of it.

The plane jolted through the sky. It was a sea of turbulence, with swirling clouds churning angrily on every side of them. They were flying deeper and deeper into a jungle of dark clouds. Marty looked around him at the dark formations and for the first time seemed to recognize he was in trouble. Pepper saw beads of sweat rise on his face and his knuckles turn white on the control wheel. Marty began whipping the plane into steep banks from side to side trying to dodge the ever-building clouds. She was scared! Her bones felt as if they had turned to jelly.

They weren't dodging the clouds anymore. One minute they were surrounded in the swirling gray mist and the next minute the plane was spiraling out of the cloud bank. In and out they went, until they were in the clouds more than they were out.

"Get below the clouds, Marty. Get down!" Pepper shouted.

"I'm trying!" he screeched.

But the grayness surrounding them didn't let loose this time. Pepper saw nothing but grayness out the windows of the plane. She could feel her body being twisted and pressed into her seat by invisible forces.

Gazing in horror at Marty, she saw that he was frozen by terror to the control wheel. The instrument panel displayed a descent of over fifteen hundred feet per minute and the wings were tipped up nearly vertical.

Pepper tried to right the plane, but Marty's hold was a death grip and she couldn't budge the wheel in any direction.

"Let loose, Marty! Let loose!" she screamed. Marty didn't flinch. His eyes stared straight ahead, his back hunched over, and his hands locked white on the black control wheel.

Pepper grabbed his wrist, trying to pull it away, but it was no use.

"Let go!" she screamed. "Let go . . . let go . . . let go . . . let go!" She pounded on his arm. Nothing. He was like a statue of granite.

Suddenly the grayness vanished as the plane shot out through the bottom of the clouds. The rush of the earth jumping up at them was terrifying. Marty screamed and flung his hands up, covering his head. Pepper instantly seized the controls, pulled the throttle back, and tried her best to level the plane out.

There just wasn't enough time. Although she leveled the plane, it wasn't enough to completely stop their descent. The plane slapped the ground a glancing blow like a flat rock skipping across the water. They had hit a wheat field and bounced a hundred feet back into the air. She struggled with the controls, but a horrible vibration shook every rivet and bolt in the plane. Pepper knew the prop had bent on impact and there would be no flying the plane to a nearby airport.

The plane slammed down two more times before sliding on its belly into a line of trees. By the time they hit the trees the plane was moving slowly. But the impact taken by the wings bent them like the swept-back wings of a jet. Pepper and Marty were flung forward against their shoulder harnesses.

All was still except for the quiet sobbing coming from Marty and Pepper's gasping for breath. Then, as if she finally understood what her danger had been, Pepper screamed.

She couldn't control herself. She screamed and tore at her seat belt in a panic to be loose. The harness clicked free and she flung herself at the door, straining on the handle until it popped open.

Pepper ran from the plane, without even thinking of the danger of fire. She ran as if she were escaping a nightmare, through the wheat field and through a barbed wire fence, ripping her clothes and scratching her body. It didn't matter. She ran until she fell from exhaustion in a ditch beside the road.

She lay sobbing in big whooping gulps, trembling uncontrollably. When she could cry no more she lay spent, watching the clouds drop their moisture in her face. She couldn't move.

How long she lay there she didn't know. She remembered noises and people looking down at her in the ditch. Then there was the siren, the stretcher, the men putting her into the ambulance, and eventually the hospital and being pushed down the hall. It was all so vague.

When she woke up, she was in one of the emergency rooms in the hospital and her parents were standing beside the bed.

"I . . . I'm still alive," she whispered. "Is Marty . . . is he okay?"

"By the grace of God, you're both fine," her father said in a ragged voice.

"You've been treated for shock, and the doctor says you can go home this evening," her mother told her as she dabbed at her eyes.

Pepper awoke the next morning in her own bed with only a hazy recollection of how she had gotten there. The alarm by her bed said eleven o'clock—she never slept that late. Tossing back the covers, she stared down at her legs covered with scratches and smeared with iodine. Of course! The crash. Involuntarily, she began to shiver. Hurriedly, she pulled on her clothes and went out to the kitchen.

"So you finally woke up," her mom said, rising from her chair at the table and hugging Pepper tightly. "Do you feel like some breakfast?"

"I'm not really hungry."

"You have to eat something. I'll fix you some oatmeal and toast and then it's back to bed with you. The doctor said after the shock you had, you have to stay in bed for a couple of days."

"No! Please . . . I mean . . . I don't want to stay in my room by myself."

"Then get your pillow and blanket and lie on the sofa. I'll stay here with you."

Pepper was just finishing her cereal when her father

came in from work and sat down opposite her. "You gave us quite a scare, young lady. In the future, I don't want you flying with anyone but Greg or Jeff without my permission. Is that clear?"

Pepper nodded as her eyes filled with tears. "Don't worry, because I'm never . . ."

"It's all right, sweetie, don't cry." Her father reached into his back pocket, pulled out his handkerchief, and handed it to Pepper. "I'm not angry with you," he said patting her hand. "A man from the F.A.A. is coming to talk to you in a little while. I'll come over with him."

"Am I in a lot of trouble?" Pepper asked with wide eyes.

"No, they just want to hear your side of the story."

Her father left, but returned in about ten minutes with Mr. Wagoner from the Federal Aviation Administration.

Pepper told him what had happened as calmly as she could until she got to the part about Marty freezing on the controls. "It was terrible," she said, covering her face with her hands as a shudder went through her. "He wouldn't let loose and I couldn't do anything."

"Mary Owens told us a slightly different version, but I believe you. Even if I didn't, he's still the one at fault. He had a private license two years ago which was revoked a few days after he received it for flying while intoxicated. He had also taken the plane Sunday without his father's knowledge."

Pepper gaped in open surprise. "B-but he told me that he was working on his commercial license."

"It's always a good idea to check a person's license before you go flying with him. You have no idea how many people put their lives in the hands of a supposedly experienced pilot who doesn't have the proper credentials. Some of them aren't as lucky as you.

"You won't be held at fault in this accident," Mr. Wagoner continued in a kinder voice. "You're free to continue with your lessons."

Oh, no, I'm not, Pepper thought as her father and Mr. Wagoner left. She had tried to tell her dad earlier, but he didn't give her a chance. She was never going to fly again, never! Nothing could ever make her climb into another plane.

Lying down on the sofa, Pepper buried her head into the pillow and was soon asleep.

When she awoke again it was midafternoon.

"You okay, Pep?" was the first thing she heard when she opened her eyes.

Jeff was standing in the arched doorway between the living and dining rooms with a worried expression.

"I'm fine," she said, sitting up on the sofa.

"Good. I hope you don't pull any fool stunt like that again."

"Don't worry, I won't . . . ever."

"Well, I've got to get back to work. Greg said he's coming over to see you in a little while."

Pepper could feel the blood draining from her face as Jeff left. Part of her wanted to see Greg more than anything, and the other part of her wanted to disappear before he came.

There wasn't long to worry about their confrontation. Shortly after Jeff left, she heard Greg in the kitchen talking to her mother. Pepper thought about going into the kitchen, but she felt as if she were glued to the sofa. She just couldn't bear to face Greg in front of her mother.

"She's in the living room. You can go on in," Pepper heard her mother say. "Tell her I'm running over to the office for a minute, but I'll be right back."

The moment Greg walked in, Pepper knew he was angry. His face looked as though it were chiseled from granite, and his eyes were snapping.

"How are you feeling?" he asked.

"I'm all right," Pepper answered, looking down at her clasped hands.

As Greg shoved his fists into his pockets and began pacing back and forth across the living room, Pepper had the distinct feeling that she was waiting for a volcano to erupt.

"I suppose you realize you could have been killed."

"Y-yes." Pepper shivered involuntarily at this reminder.

"I couldn't believe it when I heard about the accident," Greg said, shaking his head slowly. "I thought you had more sense! And after I warned you about Marty, too," he continued, his voice growing louder.

Hanging her head, Pepper waited for him to finish. She just didn't have any desire to defend herself. Besides, there was nothing she could say that would acquit her in Greg's eyes.

Greg stopped his pacing to look down at her. "At least you've learned a lesson that you'll never forget. I'll be back later to talk to you about your next flying lesson."

Before Pepper had a chance to tell him that she wouldn't be taking another lesson, he stamped out of the room.

She sat there silently, feeling as cold and lifeless as a porcelain figurine, while she tried to assimilate Greg's words.

After the way Greg had bombarded her, Pepper was completely surprised when he returned that evening.

She had been sitting in the living room with her parents, reading. Her father answered the door, and then he and her mom disappeared.

Greg carried in a small bouquet of daisies. Placing them on the end table at her elbow, he sat down beside her.

"I came to apologize. I shouldn't have been so hard on you this afternoon."

"It's okay," Pepper said with a shrug.

"No, it's not. I overreacted, but it really got to me to think how close you came to getting killed. You're just like a sister to me," he added with a catch in his voice as he reached over and ruffled her hair.

"I'm glad you're not angry anymore. That makes me feel better." Even if I do seem like a sister, Pepper added to herself.

"Think you'll be ready for another lesson Friday? You need to get back in a plane as soon as possible so you won't be afraid."

Pepper shook her head emphatically. "I'm never going to fly again as long as I live!"

After a long pause, Greg said, "You don't mean that. You're just upset now, but you'll change your mind in a few days. You're like me, Pepper. Flying's in your blood and you'd be miserable without it."

Pepper shook her head sadly as Greg's eyes held hers. "I was never more serious about anything in my whole life."

"Then we'll just have to do something about it."

"What do you mean?"

"I'm not sure myself, but I'll have to think of a way to make you *want* to fly again. You do plan to keep working at the airport, don't you?"

"Uh-huh, I guess so. I hadn't really thought about it,

but there's no reason not to. I can always use the money for something besides flying lessons."

"That's good for a start."

It wouldn't make a bit of difference, Pepper thought as Greg left. He acted as if she'd merely had a bad dream which would fade away in a day or so. And it wasn't a case of "want to" as he suggested. It was a matter of being terrified!

9

That Thursday when Pepper started back to work, she could scarcely stand to look at the planes. The sight of one made her knees feel weak and her stomach tremble. She was thankful she didn't have to refuel any that morning.

Jeff came strolling in at noon carrying his lunch. Sitting down on the sofa, he unwrapped a sandwich. "Mom said you were eating over here, so I decided to join you," he mumbled as he chomped down.

"That was nice of you," Pepper said, bringing her own lunch over and sitting down opposite him. "What's your motive, did you want me to do something for you or what?" she asked with a laugh.

"I can't believe it," Jeff said, shaking his head and pretending that her words had stunned him. "Can't a guy even eat lunch with his own sister without arousing her suspicions?"

Pepper shrugged and grinned. Though she and Jeff bantered constantly, she wouldn't want to trade him for a different brother.

"I'm glad you're back to normal with your unjust accusations, but seriously, there is something I want to ask you."

"What's that?" Pepper asked, narrowing her eyes in suspicion.

"Do you trust me?"

Because of the sincerity with which Jeff spoke, Pepper answered him in the same tone of voice. "Of course I do. You know that."

"Then let me take you up in the plane right now. I promise I'll just fly through the pattern once and then we'll land."

A knot of fear cramped Pepper's stomach at the suggestion of flying. "I can't, Jeff . . . I just can't."

"People who are in car accidents don't quit riding in cars. The sooner you get back in a plane, the easier it will be."

"That's easy for you to say. You weren't the one in the accident."

"How about if Dad took you up? Would you go then?"

"No, I wouldn't," Pepper said hoarsely, squeezing the words past the lump in her throat. "Now please leave me alone. I don't want to talk about it anymore."

"All right, I'll drop it for now, but if you change your mind, let me know."

She wasn't going to change her mind, but she didn't feel like arguing about it. Besides, Jeff was just trying to help.

Greg tried the same tactics when he came to the airport that afternoon. "Hi, Pepper," he greeted her warmly. "It's good to have you back to work. The place isn't the same without you around."

"Thanks. You're kind of early, aren't you?" Pepper asked. "I thought you weren't scheduled until three o'clock."

"I'm not, but I wanted to see you."

"Oh." Pepper felt every muscle in her body tense as she sensed what was coming next.

"I was hoping I could persuade you to go for a little flight with me."

"No. I wish everyone would believe me—I don't want to fly."

"I believe you, Pepper," Greg said, laying a hand on her arm. "But I also believe I can help you change your mind if you'll let me."

Pepper looked up into his dark eyes, warm with understanding. His hand was still on her arm, and his closeness made her heart bang against her ribs. She couldn't take her eyes from his. They were so caring that she felt as if she would cry if she didn't look away.

"Would you go someplace with me Saturday afternoon?"

Greg's question surprised her completely. Was he actually asking her for a date? "Wh-what do you mean? Where?"

"I mean, can I take you out? And the where is a surprise," he said with a grin.

"I don't know," Pepper answered. She forced her eyes away from his and stared out the window. This was probably some kind of trick to get her in a plane.

"If I promise we'll go in a car, and I won't try to get you to go flying, will you go then?"

"Well . . . okay. I guess so."

"Good," Greg answered with a pleased smile. "We'll leave about four."

For the remainder of the week Pepper found herself constantly wondering about Greg's plans. Why had he invited her to go with him? Whatever the reason, he had actually asked her for a date and she could hardly wait until four o'clock on Saturday afternoon. If only he kept his promise about not trying to get her to fly, everything would be perfect.

It seemed strange on Saturday to walk with Greg to his red Chevy instead of to an airplane.

"You look nice," Greg said, as he held open the door for Pepper.

She smiled her thanks, happy that she had decided to wear a dress.

"Are you going to tell me where we're going yet?" Pepper asked when Greg pulled the car out of the parking area.

"No way. It won't be a surprise if I do."

She stole a quick glance at Greg as he pulled the car out on the interstate and headed south. He looked so handsome in his light blue duck pants and plaid western shirt. She would be happy going anywhere with him. "As long as it doesn't have anything to do with flying," she told him, "I know I'll have a nice time."

"Now hold on just a minute," Greg said, furrowing his brow. "I didn't say this had nothing to do with flying. I only said I wouldn't try to get you in a plane."

"Oh, no," Pepper moaned. "But I thought, I mean . . ."

"Just relax," Greg said in a gentle voice. "We'll have a nice time. Wait and see."

There was a concerned look and something else in his eyes that Pepper couldn't identify which eased her anxiety. "Okay. I'll do my best."

"Good."

They rode the rest of the way in a comfortable silence. When Greg came to the last stoplight in the small town of Henrietta, he turned west.

"You're heading for the airport," Pepper said. At the same time as she spoke the words, she saw two hot-air balloons rising in the distance. One was a bright orange banded with blue stripes, the other gold dotted with large black spots. "Aren't they pretty," she said. "What is this, an air show or something?"

"You guessed it. It started at noon, but it's not over until late, so we'll still have time to see plenty."

Pepper leaned back in the seat. There was the barest whisper of sound as she let out her breath in relief. Maybe this would be fun. If nothing else, just spending the time with Greg would be fantastic.

When they arrived at the airport, Greg maneuvered the Chevy into a narrow parking space in a long line of cars. Pepper felt as if they were going to a circus instead of an air show. There were even some rides set up at one end of the terminal. A holiday mood seemed to prevail as they climbed out of the car and followed a crowd of people toward the main building.

"Glad you came?" Greg asked, smiling down at her.

Pepper nodded. "It looks like fun."

"Maybe I'll even get you to ride the Ferris wheel with me."

"Maybe so."

A high-pitched whine of an aircraft engine screamed in from the south. Heads all around them bobbed up and instinctively Pepper's chin shot up too.

Three tiny biplanes raced low over the field trailing red smoke. At the south boundary of the field, they began twisting through the air like a giant corkscrew. It was as if their wings were welded to each other as they rolled over and over twisting the red smoke into spirals like a tangle of ribbons streaming behind. Then the planes gyrated northward until they were out of sight.

Though her knees felt momentarily wobbly, she had actually enjoyed the spectacle.

"You okay?" Greg asked, studying her face.

"I'm fine."

"Then let's go watch the 'Glue Daubers.' They should be starting their show right now."

"What are they?"

"It's a club in Tulsa. The members build radio-controlled planes. They put on shows all over."

"Radio-controlled planes?" Pepper asked dubiously.

"Doesn't sound too exciting, I know, but just wait."

When they arrived at the runway, the radio-controlled planes were already buzzing around over the field doing aerobatics.

"They are pretty good," Pepper admitted after they watched for a while.

Along the side of the runway, in the grass, a man started pushing a small lawn mower. Pepper didn't think much about it until the lawn mower started going faster, leaving the man behind. As he ran to catch up with it, she realized this performance was part of the show. Suddenly, the lawn mower took off and began to fly. The man acted as if he were shocked, and the crowd roared with laughter.

Pepper and Greg laughed, too. Their eyes met and a curious warmth seemed to speak between them. "Come on," Greg said lightly, grabbing Pepper's hand and pulling her through the crowd. "It's time for the Ferris wheel."

"Already? Don't you want to watch the next show?" She couldn't help feeling surprised that Greg would opt for a Ferris wheel ride over anything to do with flying.

"I think it would be better for you if we didn't," he said.

"Why's that?"

"It's a guy doing aerobatics and he really thrills the

crowds. I want you to have a nice time, not be scared to death.'' The attentive sound of Greg's voice and the pressure of his hand holding hers sent a tremor of excitement through Pepper. His hand was firm and strong, and she wished they could stay like this forever.

"Thank you, Greg,'' she whispered, the words catching in her throat.

He must like me, she thought, as they walked on to the ticket booth. Otherwise he wouldn't act so interested and concerned about my feelings. The realization put a new bounce into her step.

Greg bought the tickets and the man operating the Ferris wheel stopped the machine to let them climb aboard. Once they were settled, Greg stretched out his arm behind her on the back of the seat. Pepper had never been so conscious of anything before as she was of Greg's nearness as they began to move slowly—up, up, and around.

They went around several times, when the machine stopped with a jolt as they reached the top. Greg smiled at her and brushed a stray lock of hair off her forehead.

"Having a nice time?'' he asked.

Pepper nodded, not willing to trust her voice.

"I hoped you would,'' Greg said, lowering his arm from the back of the seat to her shoulders and squeezing slightly.

Pepper felt as if she were enmeshed in a web of happiness. She couldn't breathe or move as Greg's eyes held hers. He was going to kiss her, she felt certain, and then the Ferris wheel lurched forward once more. They were the next ones to be let off.

The rest of their time together seemed to fly by. They watched two more shows, visited all the exhibits, and laughed over what their mothers would think of their supper—barbecue sandwiches, cotton candy, and apple cider.

Maybe he'd kiss her good night, Pepper thought dreamily as they drove back to Big Horn. But her hopes were shattered when Jeff came striding across the lawn and over to the car as Greg parked.

"I had a great time," Pepper said, smiling. If only Jeff could just disappear!

"That's good, because I have something planned for next Saturday evening, too."

"You do?" Pepper asked, her green eyes wide. "What is it this time?"

"Wait and see," Greg said with a wink. There was a pleased expression on his face as he hopped out of the car to talk to Jeff.

Pepper smiled to herself as she walked into the house. She hadn't just imagined Greg's attentiveness today or the concern in his voice. She knew she hadn't. Again and again she thought about the look that had been in his eyes while they sat at the top of the Ferris wheel. She could hardly wait to see what they would do next Saturday. Another date with Greg!

The week dragged by just as she knew it would, but the day finally arrived. When she climbed in the car with Greg that evening, he didn't start the engine immediately.

"I think I'd better tell you where we're going," he said, drumming the back of the car seat with his fingertips. "You do miss flying, don't you?"

"Well . . . yes," Pepper admitted, "but . . . I . . . still haven't changed my mind."

"I have a friend who works for Simulator Technology, Inc., and he's made arrangements for us to get into their plant tonight. You wouldn't mind doing some work in a simulator with me, would you?'' Greg asked with an earnest expression on his face.

"I-I guess not. After all, it's not the real thing. Nothing can happen.''

"That's my girl,'' Greg said as his mouth softened into a grin. "I'm not going to be happy until we have you flying again.''

Pepper hugged his words to her heart during the short drive into Big Horn. "That's my girl,'' Greg had said. They were the most beautiful words she had ever heard.

Pepper had seen the huge Simulator Technology building from the road many times, but as they parked in front of the hangar-like structure it was bigger than she had imagined.

"It's a big place, isn't it?'' Greg said. "Let's go in.''

As they walked down the sidewalk toward the back of the building, Pepper saw a man wave at Greg from the doorway of the back entrance.

"Hello, Jack,'' Greg shouted as he waved in return.

At the door Greg shook hands with his friend, a burly man over six feet tall with a full beard. Pepper figured him to be about thirty-five and, noticing the smile wrinkles around his eyes, guessed him to be full of good humor.

"Jack, I'd like you to meet one of my students, Pepper McNeil. Pepper, this is Jack Martin. He's the foreman of the second shift and a close friend of all flight instructors in the area.''

"Hi, Jack,'' Pepper said with a warm smile.

"Hi, Pepper,'' Jack said, then turned to Greg and winked. "Are you sure she's only a student?''

Greg only laughed.

"Come on in," Jack said, turning and leading them through the door of the big plant.

Their footsteps echoed through the hangar as they walked down the rows of simulators. Pepper was surprised that things were so quiet. From somewhere ahead she heard the whir of an electric drill, but other than that only an occasional murmur bounced to her from off the high walls.

"I can't believe it's so quiet in here," Pepper exclaimed.

"It's not always this quiet. Sometimes we're fabricating the bodies of the simulators and it gets a little noisy, but most all of our work is with the electronics. As the foreman, I prefer not to hear a lot of clanking and banging around when the men are putting in transistors and stringing wire."

"Good point," Pepper said with a laugh.

The simulators were much bigger than Pepper had imagined. From the cockpit forward, the simulators were identical to the planes they represented. At the back of the cockpit of each "plane" was a boxlike structure. And the whole assembly was mounted on a platform above a maze of hoses, pipes, bundled wires, and hydraulic cylinders.

"I never dreamed simulators were this complicated. I guess when you told me about using a simulator, I was thinking of one of those little ones I saw in a flying magazine that sit on a desk," Pepper said.

"These are a far cry from a desktop model," Jack said. "Most of these are Lear and Citation jet simulators. They'll cost a million dollars each."

"Wow! Why would anyone want to buy one of these if they cost so much?" Pepper asked. "I'd think they would just buy a regular plane."

"These simulators are the perfect training device; they can be put into any flight configuration without the threat of a crash. Also, they don't use any fuel. In other words, they're a lot safer and cheaper to operate," Jack explained.

"Neat," Pepper said.

"What have you got going tonight, Jack?" Greg asked, rubbing his hands together in anticipation. "Are any of the Lear jets operational?"

"No," Jack said, holding his hands up in surrender. "Please remember that we build them here and only the ones that are almost ready for shipment are operational. No Lears tonight. But we do have a Cessna Conquest ready. Come with me."

Jack led the way down the aisle and stopped at a bank of computers that were lined up between two Conquest simulators. He picked up a computer disc and slipped it into one of the big machines facing him.

"That should get us going. Come on up."

Jack preceded them up an aluminum stairway into the box behind the cockpit. "The instructor sits here in front of this computer screen. He can type in any command he wants. He can make the poor pilot fly with only one engine, ice hanging on the wings, in a tornado, and with the fuel about gone. Oh, the joys of an instructor," he said, laughing.

Pepper had only glanced at the instructor's seat in front of the computer. Her attention was fully focused on the maze of switches and gauges on the dash and console of the Conquest. The cockpit was dim and the windshield black. But as she was looking, the windshield flashed on and she saw the lights of an airport all around her.

"Oh, Greg, look!" she said excitedly, grabbing his arm.

"That's the St. Louis airport at night, folks," Jack explained.

"It's beautiful. But why is it like that?"

"Just watch," Greg said, sliding into the pilot's seat.

To Pepper's amazement Greg went through the procedures of starting the plane and it actually sounded as if that were exactly what was happening.

"Sit down in the co-pilot's seat, Pepper. Enjoy the ride," Greg said.

Pepper stepped around the console and sat in the right seat. She watched Greg move the power levers forward and the lights of the airport moved as if they were taxiing toward a runway.

"I can't believe this. I just can't believe it. It's so real!" Pepper said, her eyes wide with excitement.

Greg taxied into takeoff position on the runway and rotated the power levers full forward. A high-pitched whine of engines blared over a back speaker and the lights on the windshield shot at them, passing beneath and on either side. In Pepper's mind they were not in a simulator, but in an airplane taking off from the St. Louis airport.

Suddenly the delight on Pepper's face froze, and she felt as if her blood had turned to ice. The big hydraulic cylinders beneath her were raising the nose, shoving her back in her seat. She was flying. She knew she wasn't, but every fiber in her body told her she was. In the dimness of the cockpit she knew Greg couldn't see her, and she was glad. She didn't want to spoil his fun.

Pepper tried to look away, but she couldn't keep her eyes from the screen. It was as if her eyes delighted to torture her emotions. She would endure, for Greg.

Greg took the plane around the lights of the city and back for a landing. Pepper finally forced her eyes closed. The lights rising to meet her were too much.

"Great, Jack," Greg boomed in triumph after bringing the plane in for an excellent landing. "It's just incredible."

"You think that's something, let me show you a really fun trick," Jack said.

Greg climbed out of his seat, trading places with Jack. Pepper noticed how happy the two men were and hated to let them know that she had had enough. She felt trapped in the co-pilot's seat. It was no easy thing to slip in and out of. If she did what every emotion in her was crying to do, she'd be sitting back in Greg's car in ten seconds.

When Jack was settled in the pilot's seat once again, Pepper saw the power levers slide forward and the lights of the runway race past. Maybe she was being too childish. Surely she could understand that they were still on the ground and only playing a game. Surely she could leave her eyes open and enjoy the wonders of an electronic marvel.

Once in the air Jack circled over the lights of St. Louis and aimed the plane in a direct line toward the great arch. Though her heart was pounding uncontrollably, she was amazed at the detail the computer programmers went to to make every thing realistic. As they approached the arch, Jack lowered the plane closer to the city lights. Down they came until suddenly Pepper knew what Jack was going to do. He was going to fly under the arch. Pepper grabbed the sides of her seat and dug her fingernails into the upholstery. Why had she agreed to come?

The lights of the arch zipped past them overhead and

they were through. Pepper, unable to escape the unreasonable feeling of reality, sucked in great gulps of air trying to restrain the tears that she knew were imminent.

"That's amazing, Jack! This is better than anything I've done in a long time." Greg was enjoying himself all right, Pepper thought. She bit her lower lip and determined that she wasn't going to spoil his fun.

"You think that was something, watch this." Jack settled in his seat once more and headed the airplane toward downtown St. Louis. This time, instead of slowly lowering the plane, Jack pitched it forward into a steep dive directly toward the tallest building in sight.

Pepper's nails dug deeper into the seat cushion until there was no more strength left in her. They were racing toward destruction at three hundred miles per hour. She bit her lip until it bled, then, unable to control her emotions any longer she gave a piercing wail, shaking her head in terror. "No! No! No!"

She reached out like a cornered animal and clawed at Jack's hand, desperately trying to pull his hands from the control wheel. "Let go, don't crash! Pleeeease let go!"

"It's okay," Jack said calmly, switching off the simulator. "We're not going to crash."

"I'm sorry," Pepper said, sobbing into her hands. "It's just that——"

"It's my fault," Greg interrupted. "I should have stopped you. Pepper was in a bad plane crash a few weeks ago," he explained.

"I'm sorry, kiddo," Jack said. "I wouldn't have scared you for anything in the world."

"I—it . . . just seemed . . . so real."

"Come on," Greg said, helping her to her feet. "I'm sure you'd like to get out of this contraption."

After they climbed down from the simulator and told Jack good-bye, Greg put his arm around Pepper's shoulders and they walked outside.

"You're shaking," Greg said, holding her tighter as the metal door clanged shut behind them. "I'm sorry I was so thoughtless. I feel like a real clod."

"It's okay . . . really," Pepper stammered. "I wanted you to have a nice time, b-but . . ." To her embarrassment the tears started to fall again. As much as she wanted to stop, she was powerless to control them. Thank goodness they were the only two people outside the building.

"Try not to think about it," Greg said gently. He wrapped his hard, muscular arms around her and drew her head down to his shoulder. "It's okay," he whispered, stroking her hair lightly with his fingertips.

She cried until all that was left was a sniff and an occasional intake of breath.

"Feel better?" Greg asked at last.

Pepper nodded, suddenly very conscious of Greg's arms still around her. She wondered if he could hear her heart pounding in her chest. If he did, maybe he would think it was from fright. "Better," she told him, "but stupid."

"There's no reason for you to feel badly about the way you reacted tonight, and don't you forget that," he said in a husky voice.

With one hand, he tilted her chin up until she was looking at him. Pepper held her breath as she stared into his dark, understanding eyes. The slightest movement might break the spell. Her excitement was so strong that she felt weak all over.

Slowly Greg lowered his head and, just as she had anticipated, his lips came down on hers. His kiss was sweet and tender, and as gentle as the touch of his hand had been on her hair. In the fleeting moment that their lips touched, Pepper found herself filled with absolute wonder.

"We might as well go home," Greg said, moving away and wiping a tear off her cheek with his thumb.

If she could only know why he had kissed her, Pepper thought as they drove home. Was it just because he was trying to comfort her? She hoped that wasn't the reason. She wished he would kiss her again—but only because he wanted to.

10

"Honestly, Pepper, you don't even seem like the same person anymore," Linda exclaimed. She leaned back on the sofa in the lounge, folded her arms, and studied Pepper with a thoughtful expression.

"I don't know what you're talking about. I'm still me." She tried to laugh off Linda's remark, but she knew her laugh didn't sound very convincing.

"Oh, yes you do. When you first told me you were never flying again, I thought it was the greatest thing I'd ever heard. Boy, was I ever wrong! That's like Van Cliburn saying he's decided to quit playing the piano."

"I don't think it's quite that serious."

"Yes it is." Linda's long blond hair bounced as she nodded her head for emphasis. "I don't know how to explain it, but it's just . . . well . . . kind of as if a part of you has died or something."

Pepper didn't say anything, but chewed on her bottom lip as Linda continued.

"Listen, Pepper, if you'll start flying again, I promise I'll go up with you when you get your license."

"You're a real friend," Pepper said softly. "When I know how you feel about flying, and after the crash and all . . ."

"That wreck wasn't *your* fault. I know you'd be a dependable pilot."

"I really appreciate what you're saying, but . . ." She lifted her hands and dropped them in a helpless gesture.

"It's okay, you don't have to worry about it now," Linda said. "Just remember—when the time comes, I'm game."

Pepper merely nodded her head. She was so tired of trying to explain to people, and no one seemed to understand.

And yet Linda had really understood more than Pepper had given her credit for, she realized as she thought about the matter. Pepper presumed it was still the shock of the plane crash that made her feel so listless. But that wasn't it at all! Linda was right—it was as though a part of her had died. Pepper thought the day she received the results of her written test and found she had made a 95 was the worst one of her life. She would have been so proud if she had received the results before the accident, but with things as they were, she just felt more miserable. The longing to fly again had begun that very day.

It had been over a month since she had flown and she'd never missed anything so badly in her life! The terrible yearning made her feel an almost physical pain every time she looked at an airplane. But the fear was still there, too. How could it be possible to pine for something that scared you to death?

"Anything wrong?" Jeff asked as he walked into the lounge from the hangar. "You look as if you'd lost your best friend."

"I didn't," Pepper answered, trying to keep her voice light. "My best friend was here just a minute ago. She's not lost at all."

Jeff had been so considerate lately, but she couldn't

stand any more sympathy. She was glad when Greg came in from the other direction.

"Ready to plan our flight?" Greg asked as he spread a chart on the counter and took out his plotter and computer.

"You bet," Jeff said, coming over to join him.

"Where are you guys going?" Pepper asked with a spark of curiosity.

"Crazy—you want to come?" Jeff said with a grin.

"Aw, come on. I'm serious." She'd had no idea they were planning a trip and felt a little hurt that neither of them had mentioned it.

"We're entering the Sooner Air Classic," Jeff said.

"What's that?"

"Remember the information about the race you copied down for me when we went to White Horn Cove? It's that one, and Jeff and I are entering as partners," Greg explained.

"Really? How come you guys never said anything about it?"

"Didn't think you'd be interested," Jeff told her.

"Oh. Well, uh . . . mind if I watch you plan the trip?"

"Suit yourself," Greg murmured distractedly as he and Jeff turned their back to her and bent over the chart.

"We start here," Greg said, pointing at a spot, "fly to here, then return to where we started." He traced a line with his finger.

Pepper stood on her tiptoes and tried to see over Jeff's shoulder, but she couldn't tell where Greg was pointing.

"We'll have to stop for fuel twice," Greg continued.

"How about here and here?" Jeff asked, doing the pointing this time.

Greg nodded and Jeff scribbled something down on a sheet of paper. Once again Pepper tried to see what was going on, but Jeff's arm blocked her view.

Phooey, she might as well fill the pop machine instead of trying to see what those two were doing. They acted as if she didn't even exist, she thought as she trudged over to the storage room, unlocked it, and took out two cases of pop. After unlocking the machine, she opened it and stuck the cans in.

Then, since it was quitting time, she decided to go on home. She had all her work finished and Jeff and Greg would never miss her, that was for certain. Sure enough, they didn't even notice when she walked out the door.

An empty pop can lay outside the lounge door and Pepper kicked it all the way home. She couldn't really blame the boys for acting the way they did. After all, she'd asked for it. She was the one who told them she never wanted to fly again. But that didn't mean she wanted to be left out of everything, especially by Greg!

She couldn't help getting her hopes up after he kissed her that Saturday. In fact, she could hardly think of anything else. Every time she remembered the sweet touch of his lips on hers, she floated in a thrilling warmth that spread to every cell in her body.

But today he had ignored her and that hurt so much she could hardly stand it. Maybe flying was the only thing that made Greg interested in her, and he'd finally decided she'd never change her mind.

With a long sigh, Pepper entered the kitchen door.

"Was that a sigh of despair or just weariness?" her mother asked as she lowered a wire basket of french fries into the deep-fat fryer.

"Both, I guess. What's for supper?"

"Your favorite—cheeseburgers. One of your favorite people is going to eat with us, too."

"If you mean Greg, he and Jeff as so busy planning their old air race, he doesn't even know I'm alive."

"So that's what's wrong with you," Mrs. McNeil said with a shrewd look on her face.

"It doesn't matter to me," Pepper mumbled as she took the dishes out of the cupboard to set the table.

"I thought we'd grill the hamburgers outside," her mom said. "They always taste better that way. I'll go light the fire now, and the charcoal ought to be about right when the guys come in."

By the time the charcoal was ready, they still hadn't shown up. Pepper's mother tried the intercom, but no one answered.

"They've probably got one of their machines running and can't hear," Pepper said. "I'll run over and tell them."

Pepper felt her heart drop as she went out the door. Stephanie's Corvette was parked by the fence. The only reason she ever came to the airport was to see Greg. Everything was going wrong today, she thought as she trudged out to her dad's shop.

Opening the door, she shouted above the racket. "Time to eat!"

Her father gave her an "okay" sign, and Jeff turned off the machine he was using.

Pepper walked into the lounge area, but didn't see any sign of Greg. Stepping outside, she heard Stephanie's voice coming from around the corner of the building. Although she didn't normally try to eavesdrop on other people's conversations, what she heard made Pepper stop in her tracks.

"Oh, Greg, I don't know why you have to be in an old air race."

"I've had this planned since May," Greg said in a firm tone. "I'm not going to change my mind just because you've suddenly come up with a great idea."

"I've been doing some serious thinking," Stephanie said. "I just can't see any future in our dating when I hate everything to do with flying."

"I've been thinking the same thing," Greg said.

Pepper stepped quietly back into the lounge. They might walk around the corner any moment and she certainly didn't want them to see her there. Slipping out the hangar door, she dashed to the house. Knowing Greg, he would still walk Stephanie to her car, and Jeff could holler at him from the house.

Pepper could scarcely believe she'd heard what she did. She wouldn't have to worry about Stephanie anymore! She felt as if she'd rather skip in the front door than walk.

"Hey, Jeff," she called as she went in, "you might want to wave an arm at Greg in a little while and tell him it's time to eat. I didn't see him in the lounge."

"Maybe he'll go with Stephanie instead," Jeff answered from the kitchen.

"Whatever, but it would still be polite to let him know, since he's invited to stay." Pepper had a hard time keeping the excitement out of her voice.

In a short while, Jeff yelled at Greg and he came over to eat with them as Pepper knew he would. The moment they were seated at the table, he and Jeff began talking about the air race again. Pepper felt completely out of the picture as her mother and father joined in on the conversation, too. No one directed any questions or comments about flying to her.

"I wish you would explain to me how you can think flying a Cessna One Seventy-two is going to win an air race?" Mrs. McNeil asked. "I thought that was about the slowest plane around."

"Well, Mom, you're right about a One Seventy-two being slow, but the air race has different categories, and the One Seventy-two category is the biggest," Jeff said.

"It ought to be the biggest category!" said Mr. McNeil. "There are more Cessna One Seventy-two's in this world than any other plane."

"I guess it just means that the newest plane wins, since it would be the fastest," said Mrs. McNeil. "I can't see how you would stand a chance in our plane. It's nearly four years old."

"It's not that old, Mrs. McNeil," Greg said. "Besides, with a race of this distance, cruising speed doesn't mean that much. The race is won or lost on pilot technique."

"Well, then, what makes you fellows think you have a chance?" Mr. McNeil asked with a deadpan expression.

Pepper burst out with a laugh, and choked on a french fry.

"Slap her on the back, Greg," Jeff said. "And do it plenty hard. We wouldn't want her dying on us."

"That's not necessary," Pepper said after taking a gulp of iced tea. "Just when is this big race, anyway? It sounds exciting."

"Next Friday," Jeff said.

During the remainder of the meal, Pepper stole a few unobtrusive glances at Greg. He didn't seem to be at all upset that he and Stephanie had decided to quit dating.

Later, in her room, she thought about this latest development some more. "The coast is clear," she whispered, and twirled around once in sheer happiness.

Then abruptly she sat down on the edge of the bed as

the realization struck her—Greg and Stephanie weren't dating anymore because Stephanie didn't want anything to do with flying. Pepper had been excited about nothing. As far as Greg was concerned, she was exactly like Stephanie!

Pepper was standing at the sink on Sunday evening when she heard a shout from the other room.

"Whoopee!"

It was Jeff's voice. The phone call he'd received must have been important, she thought, as she dashed into the living room with dishwater dripping from her hands.

"What's so exciting, Jeff?" Pepper asked, looking at her beaming brother. She noticed her dad sitting in his easy chair peering over the top of the evening newspaper with knowing amusement on his face.

"That was Mr. Daniels from the mechanics school. He just told me I get to take my powerplant mechanics test right here in our own shop. And best of all, the examiner is one of Dad's old friends," Jeff said, his eyes lit up with excitement. "Dad, you crafty old codger, how did you manage that trick?"

"Don't 'old codger' me," his dad said with a grin as he laid the newspaper in his lap. "All joking aside, Jeff, just because the examiner is an old friend, don't think for a moment that he will pass you simply because you're my son."

"Yeah, I know, but it makes me feel so much better knowing I get to take my test under these conditions. How did you arrange for him to be here? I thought Mr. Daniels lived in Chicago now."

"Mac was going to be in Tulsa for a mechanics refresher course he's teaching this weekend. Since he was going to be so close he gave me a call to tell me he was coming. I asked him if he could come a day early and give you the test and he said that he'd be delighted. He said he always did want to get back at me for all the hard times I gave him when we worked together," Mr. McNeil said merrily.

"Oh, great, that's real encouraging. He's already planning to flunk me," Jeff said with a laugh.

In the meantime Pepper had grabbed a dish towel and was drying her hands when suddenly she realized that Jeff would be taking his test on Friday.

"Jeff, you can't take your test Friday, that's the day of the air race!"

The merriment vanished from Jeff's face and was replaced by a look of horror. The room became silent as he slowly turned to face his sister.

"The air race, Jeff," Pepper said softly.

"Oh, no! What will I tell Greg?"

"Don't worry about Greg," Mr. McNeil said. "He can handle that air race by himself without a hitch."

"But Dad, the rules say there must be two pilots aboard. It's such a long trip and so many planes are flying that they felt it would be unsafe not to have two pilots."

"Well, he'll just have to find someone else. You're certainly not going to miss your test for an air race."

"I know that, Dad, but Greg will be disappointed. He won't go without me, I'm sure. The air race is the kind of fun thing you do with a friend. He's not interested in paying for all that flying just to win a prize."

Pepper felt a knot of disappointment rise in her chest. She felt sick for Greg. She knew how excited he was about the air race. But now he couldn't go, or wouldn't go. Maybe he could talk another friend into going with him, but like Jeff said, it wasn't something you wanted to do with just anyone.

Pepper returned to the kitchen, slipped her hands back into the warm dishwater, grabbed the crunchy scouring pad, and went to work scrubbing the frying pan. That air race sounded like a lot of fun. She hated for Greg to miss it.

Pepper was glad she was out refueling a plane when Jeff broke the news to Greg on Monday. She didn't think she could bear to see the letdown on his face, so she purposely dawdled around outside as long as possible.

When she finally went back inside, Greg was alone. He was standing at the counter, jotting down something in his logbook. "You very busy, Pepper?" he asked, looking up when she entered.

"Not too. Why?"

"I wanted to talk to you for a little while."

"Sure. What's up?" she said. Then she noticed the droop of his shoulders and wished she hadn't asked something so ill-timed.

"Understanding how you feel, and all . . . I don't know why I'm even asking you this, but—" Greg paused and shrugged his shoulders as if what he were about to say really didn't matter, but Pepper could tell that it meant a great deal to him.

"What, Greg?"

"Would you consider being my partner in the air race?"

"Yes," Pepper said, almost surprising herself with her answer. "I'd like to." She felt as if it were an honor for Greg to ask her this question, and yet her real reason for answering yes had to do with something much deeper. If she didn't go this time, she might never get the nerve. "But wait," she went on. "I'm only a student and I thought the rules said there had to be two pilots."

"As long as you're flying from the left seat and with your instructor, you're perfectly legal."

"I'll have to fly, too?" Pepper asked, her skin feeling suddenly clammy and her stomach tightening into a knot.

"Not unless you want to. If you just take care of some of the navigation and keep me company, it would be a big help."

"Okay," Pepper murmured, wondering what on earth she had gotten herself into. And yet she knew it was something she had to do. It's got to be Friday or never, she thought with grim determination.

"Thank you, Pepper," Greg said with a smile lighting up his face. "Believe me, I know how hard this is for you, and I appreciate it more than you'll ever know. I think it's going to make a big difference for you, too, and I want that most of all."

11

Pepper was sitting in a lawn chair in front of the airport office when the 6:00 A.M. melody of singing birds was disrupted by the familiar crunch of tires on the gravel parking lot. She turned in her seat to see Greg's red Chevy come to a stop next to the fence.

It was so still and the air so calm that she could hear the click of the car door as Greg opened it fifty yards away. She watched him as he stood up beside his car, then reached behind the seat for his briefcase. He swung the door and it shut with a cushiony clunk. He looked up and Pepper could see him smile when he saw her.

"Good morning," he said in a voice almost a whisper. It seemed he was revering the stillness of the early morning, making the moment between them intimate.

"Morning," she replied in the same softness of voice. She didn't rise from her chair. The blissfulness of the morning and Greg's smile left her body limp. She smiled, leaned her head back, and relaxed against the taut nylon strapping of the lawn chair.

Pepper listened as Greg's steps across the concrete ramp echoed against the steel doors of the hangar. Then he was beside her, looking down with smiling eyes that seemed to be saying things which didn't relate to flying.

"You look pretty this morning, Pepper," he said, not raising his voice.

He reached down, laid his hand on hers, and gave it a gentle squeeze. "Thanks for going with me."

"Thank you for asking."

"Just relax a minute while I go call the weather. I'll be right back."

"Sure," she said. Suddenly a feeling of dread came over her at the mention of weather. Uneasiness made her shudder and she had to close her eyes for a second and take a deep breath before she could look at him again.

Greg gave her hand another squeeze and was off to make his phone call. Pepper was glad he hadn't noticed her uneasiness. She wanted to conquer her fear today and she didn't want him feeling sorry for her. And she didn't want anything interfering with their time together today.

When Greg came back from using the phone she saw him stop in midstride and hunch over slightly, a pained expression flashing across his face as he grabbed his lower right side.

"Are you all right?" she asked, sitting up in alarm.

"I guess so," he said.

"What's wrong?"

"Must be a pulled muscle. Bob and I played tennis last night. I haven't done much of anything athletic for a while. I guess it serves me right for not keeping in better shape," he said, shrugging it off with a laugh. He straightened up hesitantly, then ran his fingers through his hair and took a deep breath. Whatever it was seemed to have passed.

"You look kind of pale, if you ask me. Are you sure you feel good enough to go?" she asked.

"Ah, ha! Trying to get out of our date, aren't you? Well, it won't be so easy. A little muscle strain isn't going to keep me down. You're going to have to think of a better excuse than that," Greg said with a laugh, but his humor was only on the surface and Pepper knew it.

Greg pulled up a chair and sat down beside her. "About the weather," he said, then patted her hand. "We're going to have to fly over a few clouds. Now don't get shook up."

Unfortunately, getting shook up wasn't controlled by one of those manual on-and-off switches. Her switch was one of those modern automatic kinds. And Greg's words had automatically switched it to the on position. Pepper was shook up. How could her heart be beating so fast and the blood drain from her face at the same time? She'd have to ask her old biology teacher about that next fall. Maybe she wasn't a normal person.

"Easy now, Pepper. Let me explain."

Greg was getting a lot of practice patting her hand, Pepper thought. She just wished he didn't have to bring her to the brink of panic to do it.

"There is a layer of clouds that come up from the south, extend past Tulsa, and then curve east. They get thicker as we go northeast, but at Grove, where the race starts, the weather is clear. The whole route for the race is clear and predicted to stay that way. In fact, these clouds around here are predicted to pass to the east of us by this afternoon. So it will only be a matter of slipping up over a few clouds and coming down on the other side. We'll stay in the bright blue sky the whole way. How does that sound?"

"It sounds fine, Greg." She really didn't think of

this as a lie, because anything Greg said sounded fine to her.

"All right," he said, then stood up, pulling her with him. "Let's go."

Pain streaked Greg's face as he stood and once again he grabbed for his side. He took a deep breath and, trying to sound glib, said, "I'm going to have to play more tennis or give it up completely."

While Greg did his preflight inspection, Pepper strapped herself into the left seat. Then Greg climbed into the instructor's seat and without requiring Pepper to flick a lever, he fired up the engine of the Cessna and with a quick comment on the radio, taxied toward the runway.

Pepper sat erect in her seat. Her hands involuntarily sought the sides of her seat cushion and gripped it as if the gesture would stabilize the airplane. How silly, sitting in a plane frozen in fright as if her worry would make any difference in their flight. An ostrich with its head in the ground didn't have anything on her.

Greg stopped the plane before they reached the runway. "Pepper, hand me the check list, would you? It's in that pouch by your left leg."

"Sure," she said, forcing her cheek muscles to rise into what she hoped Greg would take as a smile.

"What's wrong?" he asked. "Are you afraid already?"

Evidently her smile attempt hadn't worked. She reached down for the check list and presented it to Greg.

"No, I'm . . . all right. It's just a little hot in here right now. Once we take off and the air starts coming through vents, I'm sure I'll feel much better."

That sounded good, she thought. I've convinced him I'm fine. I'm handling this pretty well. I wanted to be with Greg and I'll be with him and he'll never know how I feel.

"Pepper?"

"Yes?" she answered with the precise inflection in her voice to sound at ease.

"Relax, we haven't even taken off yet."

"I am relaxed, Greg. Everything is fine."

"Then would you please open your white-knuckled little hand and let me have the check list?"

Her gaze shot downward and there, as if she weren't even part of her body, she saw her hand in a tug of war with Greg's. Tears welled up in her eyes. She tried to stop them by biting her lips, but the big drops trickled out and plopped on the check list.

Dropping her hands, she clamped them to the seat cushion again. At the same instant, she twisted her burning face away so Greg couldn't see her humiliation and tears.

Though the engine throbbed, there was a silence in the plane. Pepper could sense it in Greg. He made no movement and didn't speak for several minutes. Then without a word, Greg eased the throttle forward and the plane began to move. Shutting shut her eyes, she braced herself for the acceleration of the takeoff. But the acceleration never came.

She opened her eyes to peek ahead, and to her surprise found they were taxiing back to the ramp.

"Where are we going?" she asked weakly.

"We're not going anywhere. And you're going home. I didn't ask you along to torture you. I asked you to come because I thought we could really enjoy doing something together that we both cut out for. I was wrong, and I'm sorry I tried to get you to go."

"Oh please, Greg, no," she said, grabbing his arm with both of her hands. "I'm sorry I'm so stupid. I don't want you to miss the air race. I wouldn't have come if being scared was all I was worried about. I came because I had to. I can't know if I'll ever get over that crash if I don't go now, today, with you."

Greg toed the brakes, bringing the plane to a stop. He looked into her pleading eyes for what seemed like forever. Then once again without saying a word, he pushed the throttle in, turned the plane around, and headed back to the runway.

Pepper's outburst had sapped some of her rigidness and she began to relax. It wasn't so much that she was getting braver, but her mind was strangely drawn to the movements of a pilot preparing for takeoff.

It was as if it were the first time she had ever noticed how precise every motion of a professional pilot could be. She watched Greg's hands flick switches and his eyes scan the instruments with the intensity of an eagle, and listened to his clipped voice announcing their departure in just the right words. Greg was a professional, all right. Pepper felt herself loosening up. This wasn't a Marty in the other seat, it was her instructor.

The air was so calm and Greg operated the controls so deftly that Pepper didn't feel any sudden swoop as the plane left the ground. The wings didn't bobble a fraction as they sailed serenely above the tree-lined meadows surrounding the sleepy town of Big Horn. The grass, still wet with dew, sparkled in the early morning sun as though it had been sprinkled with diamonds.

She *had* missed flying—much more than she had thought. Even as they soared above the puffy whiteness of the clouds, she could feel her apprehension abating.

"You've missed it, haven't you?" Greg's words above the drone of the engine brought her out of her own thoughts.

"You mean flying?" she asked, looking at Greg for the first time since they took off.

Greg only smiled his response.

"You've been reading my mind," she said. Pepper looked down and was surprised to see her hands folded comfortably in her lap.

"I'm glad you've relaxed. I'd been thinking we would have to re-upholster your seat cushion when we got home."

Pepper smiled. Greg was really quite a guy. And the truth of the matter was that she had relaxed. In that moment, Pepper felt the tension of the last weeks unravel, leaving her light-headed in the splendor of a blue sky above a snowy carpet of clouds.

Without warning the plane dipped and Pepper turned to see Greg, bent over double, vomiting into an airsick bag. Moaning in pain, he sealed the sicksack and put it under his seat.

"Greg!" Pepper shouted. "Greg! What's wrong?"

"I don't . . . know. My side is hurting pretty bad!" he said, holding his lower right side in the same place that had bothered him before they took off.

Pepper grabbed the controls and leveled the plane, then looked at him once again. The thought passed through her mind that he was pulling a trick on her so she would fly the plane. But it only took one look to know that he wasn't faking. His body was doubled over with his hands clasping at his side, his face was contorted with agony, and his skin was pasty and beaded with sweat. She realized suddenly that he must be having an appendicitis attack.

"Greg, what do I do?"

"Just get us down. Please . . . Pepper . . . down!"

"Where, Greg? All these clouds . . . I don't even know were we are."

"Call . . . Tulsa Approach . . . on emergency frequency . . . one twenty-one point five. Tell them . . . tell them . . . what's happened. Tell them . . . emergency." Greg reached up and with a contorted hand twisted in 7777 on the transponder. Pepper knew that was the distress signal to all radar stations picking them up.

Pepper tuned in 121.5 on the radio. "Tulsa Approach Control, this is Cessna Four Nine Seven Three Gulf and I'm declaring an emergency, over."

"Roger, Seven Three Gulf, this is Tulsa Approach, what is your situation?"

Perspiration beaded up on Pepper's face and she tried to moisten her lips before pressing the mike button, but her cottony mouth wouldn't cooperate. "Tulsa, this is Seven Three Gulf. I'm a student pilot and my instructor just got sick. I think he has appendicitis or something. I don't know where I am and he needs to get to a hospital."

"Seven Three Gulf, this is Tulsa Approach. Are you in the clouds?"

"No, sir, we're above them at five thousand feet."

"Okay, fine. We'll get you down in good shape and when you land we'll have an ambulance standing ready. What's your name, young lady?"

"It's Pepper McNeil. But what should I do?" she said, exasperated at the man for asking her name at a time like this.

"Good, Pepper. I'm Tom. Now just listen to what I tell you to do and you'll get down safe and sound. Okay?"

"Okay . . . Tom," Pepper said, turning her head away from Greg, who was retching again.

"Pepper, how far along are you in your flight training?"

"Well, pretty far, except I quit for several weeks. I was almost ready to take my check ride," she said, not believing how casual this Tom was when there was an emergency to take care of.

"That's good, Pepper. I wanted to make sure you would be able to follow my instructions before I started guiding you in. But it sounds like it ought to a piece of cake for you."

"I . . . I think I can do it. I need to do it."

"All right, Pepper, turn left to a heading of north. I'm going to get you lined up with the runway about twenty miles out and let you descend through the clouds straight ahead. The ceiling here is two thousand feet so it really won't be a problem if you'll just keep your wings level as you come down through the clouds."

"Okay . . . I'm going north."

"Fine. It will be a few minutes before I'll have you turn again, so don't go to sleep on me."

"You don't have to worry about me going to sleep."

They droned on for several minutes with Tom making light conversation. Pepper now realized he was doing a good job of keeping a student pilot at ease in an emergency.

"Time to turn again, Pepper. Turn left to a heading of west."

Pepper made the turn. "I'm going west now, Tom."

"Good. Now in about one minute I'll have you turn toward the south and then you'll start descending. Does that sound too spooky?"

"I guess not. My instructor had me do a lot of flying under the hood, but I'm still kind of scared."

"Good, I'm glad to know you're human. Being scared will only make you more alert. I think you'll do fine."

"I hope you're right," she said, feeling sorry for Greg. She had to do a good job, she had to get him down in a hurry.

"Okay, Pepper, turn to a heading of south. Let me know when you're set and I'll start you down through the clouds."

She made her turn to the south, took a deep breath, and settled deeper into her seat. "I guess I'm as ready as I'll ever be."

"Fine. Now, Pepper, I want you to look at the attitude indicator and tell me if the little airplane is centered on the artificial horizon."

"Yes, it's centered," she replied.

"Great. Now, lower the nose of the plane so the ball in the middle of that little airplane is right below the horizon line."

"It's there and we're going down. I'll trim the plane so I don't have to hold the pressure."

"Hey, you're way ahead of me. Now you're all set. All you have to do is keep your eyes on the attitude indicator, making sure the little airplane stays where it's supposed to, and slip right on down to us."

"I'm getting ready to go into the clouds right now," she said breathlessly. The clouds seemed to swallow the little plane. Out the windows there was nothing but a white mist. Pepper knew if she didn't keep her eyes on the attitude indicator she could get vertigo and panic. She had to stay calm. She had to fly like she had never flown before.

"Okay, Pepper, just keep your eyes on that attitude indicator and believe it. Don't think a wing is dropping just because you feel like it. What is your altitude now?''

"Three thousand feet. I'm still nervous, but this is really pretty easy.''

"That a girl. You're just about home free. Only another five hundred feet to go.''

In another minute the clouds parted like a curtain on the opening act of a wonderful play. The grass was as green as a sea of emeralds. She had never seen a more beautiful sight in her life.

"I made it! I made it! I'm through the clouds, Tom!''

"Great, Pepper! Now, you're a little off course so if you'll turn to a course of one six five you should run right into the airport.''

"I see it! I can make it now. Is the ambulance there yet?''

"Yes, ma'am, and you are cleared to land on runway one seven right.''

"Thank you, Tom," she said, beaming with a sense of accomplishment.

"Greg, we're almost there. And the ambulance is waiting.''

"Thanks . . . Pepper . . .'' Greg said through clenched teeth.

Pepper lined up perfectly with the runway and slid the plane onto the concrete so smoothly only the squeaking of the tires told her she was on the ground.

She spotted the ambulance on the ramp off to her right. Taxiing up beside it, she pulled the mixture, killing the engine. Before the propeller had stopped spinning, the white-uniformed men from the ambulance were taking Greg out of the plane.

Pepper closed her eyes, exhausted and even trembling a little over her ordeal.

"Would you like us to help you out?" one of the attendants asked.

Pepper's eyes popped open. "I'm fine. I'll have to park the plane . . ."

"The people here will park the plane. You can come with us. I'm sure you'd like to know how your friend does."

12

Pepper couldn't sit still in the waiting room. She would sit down for a little while, glance at the clock with the second hand creeping slowly around, stand up, walk over and look out the window, then start the whole process over.

This ritual wasn't even because she was terribly worried. Greg had suffered an acute attack of appendicitis and was in surgery right now, but the doctor had assured her he would be fine.

Maybe she just had too much adrenaline in her blood, she thought as she paced the tiled floor again. So much had happened so quickly that her head still felt as if it were spinning.

She was standing by the window once more, looking down at the traffic, when the elevator opened and her mother and father stepped out. Without a word, her mom came over, gathered Pepper into her arms, and held her close.

"How's Greg?" Mrs. McNeil asked.

"He should be out of the operating room in a little while. The doctor said he would call me when it was all over." Pepper was surprised at how shaky her voice sounded now that everything was okay.

"What about you?" her mother asked, holding Pepper at arm's length and searching her face. "Are you all right?"

"I—I'm just fine."

"Your mother talked to Mrs. Connolly on the phone," her father said. "Since she's visiting her mother in Wichita and won't be able to get here for a few hours, we promised her we'd stay until Greg came out of the recovery room. Of course, we'd stay anyway."

Just then a nurse came in and told Pepper she had a call at the desk. She and her parents followed the nurse to the desk, where Pepper picked up the phone hesitantly. Greg just had to be all right.

"This is Pepper McNeil."

"Your friend made it through his surgery in great shape," Dr. Bradley, the surgeon, told her. "He's in recovery now, and you can see him in about an hour."

"Thank you."

"By the way, young lady, I hear you're something of a heroine. It's a good thing you got Greg here so promptly. A little longer and his appendix would have burst."

The hour they were forced to wait seemed to drag by, but finally they were allowed to see Greg.

Pepper tiptoed into his room first, followed by her parents. He appeared to be asleep, but then he opened his eyes and smiled weakly. "Hi, Pepper."

She walked over and clasped his hand, surprised at his strength as he gripped hers. "You've . . . got quite . . . a daughter, Mr. McNeil," he said in a thick, groggy voice, then shut his eyes and went back to sleep.

Pepper had to pry Greg's fingers from hers.

"We might as well go, hon," her mother said. "Your dad's got to get back to work."

"I was surprised you even took off work to come, Daddy," Pepper said as they left the room.

"I had to come take the plane back, since Jeff's busy."

"Oh, that's right. I forgot about the plane."

"I thought we could eat at the airport," her mother said. "Then your father can fly home and we'll drive."

"I hope I don't disappoint you, Mom," Pepper said with a grin. "I get to be with you a lot more than Dad, so I think I'll just fly with him!"

It was Monday afternoon before Pepper and Jeff went to visit Greg. His bed was in a sitting position and he looked almost like his old self.

"It's about time," he said when they walked in. "I thought you two had deserted me."

"From what your mom told us, you wouldn't have appreciated our company," Jeff said.

"It's a good thing you have an excuse," Greg said. "Well . . . don't just stand there, pull up a seat."

Jeff carried two chairs over by the bed.

"You sit here, Pepper," Greg said, motioning to the closest one.

The moment Pepper sat down, Greg reached for her hand and held it tightly. She could feel the heat rising in her face as she wondered what Jeff was thinking.

"You did a great job flying Friday. Sorry I failed to mention it at the time," Greg said with a warm smile. "I hope you weren't too scared."

"I didn't really have time to be."

"I think she's over the hump," Jeff said. "She made Dad let her do all the flying when they brought the One Seventy-two back Friday."

"That's great."

"You may not believe this," Pepper said, "but when you first got sick Friday, I thought you might be trying to trick me into flying."

"Jeff and I did have a few things up our sleeves, but that wasn't one of them."

"Such as what?" Pepper asked.

"We finally decided if we just ignored you and didn't talk to you about flying, it might really get to you," Jeff said.

"Well, you were right," Pepper admitted.

"You ought to know I wouldn't trick you into flying, though," Greg said in a gruff voice. "But, if having an appendicitis attack did the job, then I'm glad I did."

"It worked like a charm. When do I get to start my lessons again?"

"You can finish up on your solo work," Greg said, tightening his grip on her hand. "You'll only need about three more hours of instruction from me, so we both ought to be ready for that in about two and a half weeks."

"Jeff's got some news, too," Pepper said.

"Your exam!" Greg said. "How did it go?"

"Mr. Daniels gave me quite a workout, but I got through everything okay," Jeff said with a pleased expression.

"He's just being humble," Pepper said. "Mr. Daniels told Dad that Jeff was a natural."

"We need to get going, Pepper," Jeff said, looking at his watch. "Why don't I go buy us Pepsis, and meet you at the car in ten minutes?" he said to Pepper. "Take it easy," he told Greg as he walked out the door.

"I wonder what's wrong with him," Pepper said after Jeff left. "He usually sends me on all the errands."

"Maybe he knew I'd want to thank you again, with no one else around," Greg said softly. "Sit up here for a minute." He smiled at her and patted the side of the bed.

His eyes held hers as she stood up and sat down beside him, and she felt as if she were caught in a glow of delight as she tried to absorb the deliciousness of what was happening. Something in Pepper seemed to melt completely as she stared into Greg's dark, luminous eyes.

"Thanks, Pepper," he whispered, and then his arms went around her and his lips covered hers for a long magical moment.

When the kiss had ended and Pepper stood to leave, she scarcely dared to even breathe. It might break the enchantment between them. Instead of saying good-bye, she smiled, feeling certain that he would read in her face what her heart was saying. The look that passed between them told her that he did.

Pepper felt as if she were floating as she walked down the hall toward the elevator in the waiting room. But when the door to the elevator opened, she was certain her heart stopped beating.

"Pepper!" Stephanie said as she got off. "I'm so glad to see you. I just arrived home from two weeks in the Caribbean and found out that Greg is in the hospital. We had kind of a misunderstanding a few weeks ago and I feel so awful about everything," she explained in a rush. "Can you tell me how to find his room?"

Pepper felt as if she were a marionette as she woodenly lifted her arm and pointed down the hall. "Seven oh three—it's the first one on the left after the nurses' station. Y-you can't miss it."

"Thanks," Stephanie said before she hurried off.

This couldn't be happening, Pepper thought dazedly as she walked out through the blazing Oklahoma heat to the car. Everything had been working out so perfectly. She was ready to fly once more, Greg had kissed her again—and now this!

Pepper opened the door, climbed in the car, and leaned her head back against the headrest.

"You sure took long enough," Jeff said with a twinkle in his eyes.

"Yeah," Pepper agreed, scarcely hearing his words.

She remained lost in thought on the trip home, trying to assimilate what Stephanie's appearance at the hospital would mean. How could Greg possibly resist if a girl like Stephanie apologized to him? He couldn't! she decided as she stared unseeing out the window.

Pepper was thankful that she had her flying to keep her busy during the next two and a half weeks. Otherwise, she didn't know how she could cope with the feeling of loss that seemed to surround her whenever she wasn't working. She felt as if she were a robot as she went about her duties, but flying took her total concentration.

When Greg called to line her out on what she should be doing, Pepper kept her voice completely businesslike. After all, it wasn't his fault that she had a crush on him.

When she made herself analyze everything, she realized he probably only kissed her that afternoon in the hospital because he was grateful to her for not panicking and for landing the plane safely. Even if that weren't the case, Stephanie's apology would have destroyed any chance she might have had.

It was late on a Tuesday morning when Jeff ambled into the lounge. "Greg called while you were flying.

He said he would be out to give you a lesson pretty soon.''

Jeff had no sooner finished speaking than Greg walked in. As usual, her heart began banging against her ribs when he smiled at her.

"Are you sure you feel up to this?" Pepper asked.

"The doctor gave his okay as long as I don't tire myself out."

"She meant the strain of teaching *her*," Jeff said with a grin.

Pepper stuck her tongue out at Jeff and laughed. "I'll get the plane ready," she said, and dashed out the door.

If he's too nice, I'll cry, Pepper thought as she preflighted the plane. Fortunately, Greg was all business and he spent an hour and a half working her hard.

When at last she stopped the plane by the gas pumps, she leaned back with a weary sigh.

"I hope it wasn't that bad," Greg said. "We're going to have another hour and a half of this Thursday, and then you're scheduled for your test Friday."

"Really, Greg?" Pepper exclaimed, the weariness vanishing immediately. "Just in time for my birthday, like I planned all along!"

"That's right."

The lesson Thursday was a repeat of Tuesday's workout. This time when they finished, they went in the lounge and Greg signed Pepper's logbook and a recommendation form for her to take her check ride.

"I'm sending you to Mr. Bohanan in Ardmore," he said as he clicked his ballpoint pen shut and stuck it into his pocket.

"I just hope I pass."

"You'd better. There's a celebration planned."

Her folks must be giving her a surprise party and had

invited Greg, Pepper decided. He'd better watch out. He'd almost given it away.

"You're not really worried, are you?" Greg asked with genuine concern on his face.

"I—I guess not. It's just hard to believe the time to take my check ride is almost here," she said as she tapped her fingers on the glass counter.

"You're going to do great," Greg said, placing his hand over hers. The warmth of his hand seemed to send an electrical shock up her arm, and she felt completely flustered.

When Pepper landed at Ardmore the next afternoon, she could feel her knees wobbling as she walked to the office where she was supposed to meet her examiner.

She found the office without any trouble and was surprised to see Salty when she peeked in the door. "Why, Salty, hi," she said, a smile spreading across her face. "I'm looking for my examiner. I'm ready for my check ride. His name is Mr. Boha——" Pepper stopped in midsentence and her mouth gaped open in astonishment. "Salty Bohanan? Isn't that what you said your name was? I didn't even connect the two."

"I didn't recognize the name Patricia myself when your instructor called," Salty said, his eyes wrinkling merrily at the corners.

"Wow," Pepper said with a sigh of relief. "I feel better already. Not that I think you'd let me get by," she explained quickly.

He didn't either. Mr. Bohanan made Pepper perform every maneuver she knew, and then some. But still there was an affinity between them which put her completely at ease.

When Pepper landed the last time and taxied from the

runway, she did so knowing she had flown her best. It didn't really come as a surprise to her when Salty took her into the office and typed out a white pilot's certificate. "What are you plans now that you've got this?" he asked with a smile.

"Save my money and work on my instrument rating," Pepper responded immediately.

Salty nodded as if in agreement. "Thanks for keeping your promise, Pepper," he said as he walked her to the door.

"What's that?" she asked in surprise.

"The last time you were here, you said you'd come back to see me."

"That's right," Pepper said with a laugh. "I did, didn't I?"

Pepper felt as if she were a conquering hero when she returned home and found her whole family and Greg waiting outside the lounge. She could see them all waving as she circled the airport to land.

When she pulled up to the gas pump, she hopped out, waving her white slip of paper.

"I'll take care of the plane," Jeff said, thumping her on the back and grinning from ear to ear.

When they walked over to the house a few moments later, Pepper wasn't surprised to see a birthday cake sitting on the supper table.

After supper and a happy time of comparing private check rides with her dad, Jeff, and Greg, everyone went into the living room so Pepper could open her presents.

Her parents' gift was a leather logbook with her name imprinted in gold, Jeff presented her with a T-shirt that said "World's Greatest Female Pilot," and Greg gave her a necklace with a tiny gold plane.

When the gifts had all been opened, everyone drifted

away, leaving Pepper and Greg alone in the living room.

"I hope you don't have anything planned for tomorrow evening," Greg said, coming over to sit beside her on the sofa.

"No, why?"

"I told you Thursday there was a celebration lined up, remember?" he said, taking her hand. The familiar hot and cold tingle inched its way up Pepper's spine.

"I thought this was it!"

"I have your parents' permission to fly you to Shangri-La for dinner tomorrow evening."

Shangri-La, the fanciest resort in the state, set on the shores of Grand Lake . . . Pepper thought happily of her green dress waiting in the closet for such an occasion. "W-why, Greg?" Pepper asked in a quavery voice, then immediately felt foolish asking him such a question.

"Because I happen to think you're very special. I always kind of thought of you as a kid sister, even while I was teaching you to fly. But after you had that crash, I began to realize how close I really felt toward you. By then, I was pretty certain you felt the same way. I would have told you all of this while I was in the hospital, but I didn't want to throw off your test in any way."

"There's only one thing, Greg," Pepper said, dropping her eyes. She couldn't bear to look at him, but she had to find out. She had to know before she could be really happy. "What about Stephanie?"

"She's nice enough," Greg said seriously, "but we aren't dating anymore. We just aren't each other's type."

Pepper's eyes flew to Greg's and she felt captured by their warmth.

"Who is your type?" Pepper asked with a teasing gleam in her eyes.

"If you don't know after the little speech I just made, I'm not going to tell you," Greg answered. Then he leaned over and Pepper could feel the happiness rising inside her as his lips brushed hers in a soft, sweet caress.

About the Author

Sandy Miller lives and works on a boys' ranch in Oklahoma with her husband and six children. She is also the author of TWO LOVES FOR JENNY, which was made into an ABC Afterschool Special called "Between Two Loves," and SMART GIRL. Both books are available in Signet Vista editions.

SIGNET VISTA Books for Your Library

*Prices slightly higher in Canada

Buy them at your local

bookstore or use coupon

on next page for ordering.

Great Reading from SIGNET VISTA

JOIN THE SIGNET **VISTA READER'S PANEL**

Help us bring you more of the books you like by filling out this survey and mailing it in today!

1. The title of the last paperback book I bought was:
   _____

2. Did someone recommend this book to you?
   (Check One) ☐ Yes ☐ No
   If YES, was it a ☐ Friend ☐ Teacher ☐ Librarian ☐ Parent.
   If NO, did you choose it because of: ☐ the cover ☐ the author
   ☐ the subject ☐ other: _____

3. Would you recommend this book to someone else?
   (Check One) ☐ Yes ☐ No

4. How many paperback books have you bought for your own
   reading enjoyment in the last six months?
   ☐ 1 to 3 ☐ 4 to 6 ☐ 7 to 10 ☐ 11 to 15 ☐ 16 or more

5. I usually buy my books at (Check One or more):
   ☐ Bookstore ☐ Drug Store ☐ Dept. Store ☐ Supermarket
   ☐ Discount Store ☐ School Bookstore ☐ School Bookclub
   ☐ School Book Fair ☐ Other:_____

6. Have you recently borrowed any paperback books from
   your: (Check One or More) ☐ Friends ☐ Parents
   ☐ Public Library ☐ School Library

7. What other paperback titles have you read in the last six
   months? Please list titles:_____
   _____
   _____
   _____

8. Who are your three favorite authors? _____
   _____
   _____

9. Do you read magazines regularly? (Check One) ☐ Yes ☐ No
   Please list your favorite magazines:_____
   _____

For our records, we need this information from all our Reader's
Panel members.
Name:_____
Address:_____ Zip _____
Telephone: Area Code (   ) Number_____

10. Age (Check One): ☐ 10 to 11 ☐ 12 to 13 ☐ 14 to 15
    ☐ 16 to 17 ☐ 18 and over

11. Check One: ☐ Male ☐ Female

12. I am a: (Check One) ☐ Student ☐ Parent ☐ Librarian
    ☐ Teacher

13. I enjoy reading (Check One) ☐ Fiction ☐ Nonfiction books
    about (Check One or more): ☐ Friendships ☐ Romance
    ☐ Sports ☐ Humor ☐ Mystery/Adventure ☐ Science Fiction
    ☐ Teenage Problems ☐ Other:_____

Thank you for your help! Please mail this to the address listed
below.

NEW AMERICAN LIBRARY EDUCATION DEPARTMENT
1633 BROADWAY, NEW YORK, N.Y. 10019